Enticing Aurora

INDULGE ME

ALIE GARNETT

12-153-44 PUBLISHING

CHAPTER

One

LYING IN BED, Aurora Carlyle looked at her phone closely, knowing she should switch to her laptop for its larger screen, but that was down the hallway on the kitchen table. Way too far away and she wasn't getting up. So, the phone it was. So small and unreadable. Groaning, she grabbed at the reading glasses on the bedside table, pushing them on, and everything became clear.

Cursing softly into the semi-dark room, Aurora was not admitting to getting old. She wasn't even forty yet; she didn't need reading glasses. But lately, the glasses had started to work so well for seeing small things.

After a quick check of her work messages, she surfed the web for a while. When nothing interested her, she tapped on the forbidden Indulge app that was still on her phone. Not that it was anything nasty, well, maybe a little. It was a hookup app she and Win had signed up for two years before. For Win, it had brought an adoring husband and his son into her life.

It had been the exact thing Aurora had wanted for her best friend and neighbor. Not the kid part, but that had been a little happy bonus. That kid was Aurora's favorite part of Daniel McIntosh. The man himself was nice enough, just not Aurora's type. But she and Win had never had the same taste in men.

Once Indulge was open, she looked for any communication from John82. *Nothing.* Closing the app, she tossed the phone on her bed. There never was. It had been almost two years, and she was never going to find him. John was not his name, Aura was not hers, they had met three times, and Aurora had ended it, per her own self-imposed rule of three and done. It was supposed to be just a hook-up, just clean, fun sex. But that man had rocked her soccer mom world. Okay, she was no soccer mom, but he didn't know that. Men actually had some big expectations when you own a strip club or two. Ones she could meet every day of the week, but didn't want to sometimes.

At the time, she had been in the middle of purchasing her fifth club. She was climbing that mountain of success right to the top. In just five years, she had five clubs and was looking around at others. There was no stopping her.

Until she was stopped dead in her tracks, all because of John. But he didn't know that. He just walked out of her life and kept going on with his own. Aurora would have been jealous of him if it hadn't been for the one thing he left behind. *Millicent.*

At thirty-five, Aurora hadn't been pleased or even believed that the condom had failed. In twenty years, she hadn't had that happen once, or at least had it happen, and got knocked up. Then she had panicked for about a week, trying to reconnect with the guy on Indulge with no luck. She had even thought about a private detective, but she didn't have much info to give one of those. She'd puked more than a few times, and it wasn't the morning sickness.

Back then, she had been a successful business woman who owned her own apartment, a downtown penthouse on the top floor. At the time, she had never thought about children, *never.* Other people had children, not Aurora Carlyle. That hadn't changed in a single moment. It had actually taken a lot of time and thought to get to that moment. But by the time her doctor put that wiggling mass covered in yuk on her chest, she loved her. Millie was her life now, and she wouldn't trade her for all the strip clubs in the state.

Now, the little thing was over a year old, and if Aurora hadn't been there herself, she would swear it wasn't hers. No blond hair like her momma on this little lady, but thick black hair from day one. Which was why she'd named her Millicent *Winter* Carlyle, pissing off her friend, Winter Rose Knight, who thought *Winter* was a stripper name. But it was a name Aurora had always secretly loved.

Sure, Winter had been a stripper, and so had Aurora. At eighteen, when they were both booted from the system, they'd had nothing and no one. They were homeless, jobless, and hungry. That was the combination Aurora looked for in her girls. That and a determination to be more. Both she and Winter and had that determination. When they walked into the strip club, they both already had scholarships to the state college in town, but they had months before they could move into the dorms. That summer, they lived at the club in a back room.

Seven years later, they graduated with their master's degrees in business. A couple of strippers did that. They stripped the entire time, paying for school with scholarships and small bills. Neither were ashamed of the fact, even if they didn't advertise it either.

Win went to corporate America, and Aurora really kind of stayed where they were. In the beginning, Aurora said it was what she wanted, but now she could see how scared she was to walk away from the seedy underbelly of the city. It was all she knew.

Not that being a stripper was the same thing as owning the club, but for Aurora, the line was very shallow. Her happy place was inside a good titty bar. Not that tits were her thing, but she could appreciate some good ones. And now she knew how to market the shit out of them.

At thirty, she had been managing five bars, all strip clubs. It was good money. Win never could believe that Aurora could pull down that kind of money. But Win had easily forgotten how much the cops and feds were always looking down at clubs because there was so much crime in a lot of them. Aurora's job had been to keep the records squeaky clean and the business running smoothly. For that, she was paid handsomely. When her friend, Sparkle, not her real name, had offered her ownership of the club that had supported both her and Win through college, Aurora jumped at the chance.

One club had turned into two and then to five. But then Millie came, and five became four and would soon settle into two. Her daughter was her everything now.

She would like to think no one who looked at her would think she was a stripper, but she would be lying to herself about that. She was blessed with a stripper body, big tits, a large round ass, and platinum blond hair. Only one of those was fake. She was born a dirty blond. What people couldn't see was that she wasn't some dumb blond. She was a college graduate. Hell, she had her master's in business.

Her phone rang in her hand, scaring her enough that she dropped it and had to dig in the covers to find it again. She hoped it was Win but was disappointed when it was the club—and not her favorite one. It was called Bottoms Up and was cheesy as hell, but business was good, so she left it as it was.

"It's Aurora," she answered as always.

Not many people had her number, and those who did knew who they were calling.

"We have an issue with one of the girls. Big fight with a customer," Trish said.

She was the club's night supervisor. A woman whom Aurora had known for years and would trust with almost anything at this point.

"Is she okay?" Aurora asked. Her first concern was always for those she employed. They were always the top priority. They were hers to protect.

"Both of the women are fine," Trish said. "But you might want to come down."

Both were women? Women were rarely the issue in her clubs. Not because they didn't visit but because they didn't have the testosterone rushing through their veins that made them do stupid things.

"I'll be down in half an hour."

Aurora hung up the phone. If she wasn't needed there, they wouldn't have called. Her employees could handle a lot of shit before calling her.

Tossing her glasses back on the nightstand, she reluctantly crawled out of bed, shedding the silk pajamas she liked to wear. Tonight's were a cheery yellow. Slipping on a pencil skirt and a red blouse, she decided she had been spending too much time with Win, except Win would have a jacket and heels to match. That was just how Win was and always had been.

Grabbing a pair of well-loved black heels, she slipped her phone into her pocket and shut off her bedroom light just as the clock struck two a.m. In Millie's room, she picked up the dark-haired baby and hoped the little thing wouldn't wake up as she left her apartment. Letting go of her heels, they fell silently to the carpeted hallway as she unlocked the door across the hallway.

In Win and Daniel's apartment, she put the baby in the little crib by the front door. This wasn't the first time a midnight call had come in. Win would be excited to see the baby come morning. Knowing exactly why she was there—because even if Aurora was back before the time the couple next door got up, she would leave Millie with them. There was no need to risk waking her twice.

Kissing her love, she returned to the hallway and slipped her shoes to tackle the issue at the club. It never used to bother her to go out in the middle of the night, but with Millie, she hated being super tired when she had her time with the baby in the mornings.

Taking the elevator to the underground garage, she pulled out her keys, only then realizing that she had only grabbed her apartment keys in her haste. Cursing, she decided to do what anyone would do in that situation. She would just take Win's car.

Years before, when they decided they had finally made it, they had purchased top-floor units in a high-rise across the hall from each other. Aurora's bright red BMW was always parked next to Win's 1990s classic brown Buick. Win never drove it; she worked two blocks away, and Aurora or Daniel always drove when they went somewhere. The car was mostly used to leave at the airport when they went on trips. Since Daniel had moved in, they had purchased another parking spot. Aurora never understood why Win was so attached to that brown car.

The car was never locked. Win was not scared it would be stolen in their underground parking garage. Inside, it was dusty and dirty from years of being down here. With nimble fingers, she quickly hot wired the car. Once it was running, she let it idle some to get used to running again, remembering its job.

Aurora had hot-wired her first car at eight, but she had been in training since she was born. In fact, it was only when she was six and attending a birthday party for a classmate at school that she witnessed a car being started with a key for the first time. Ever.

The man in her mom's life for most of Aurora's early years ran a chop shop. Her mom and grandma were always getting him cars. Or sometimes just something for themselves when they needed a vehicle. The 90s Buick had been hot-wired more than it had been started with a key since Win got it. But Win never drove it.

Pulling out of the parking garage, Aurora realized she missed her luxury SUV. Win's car stank. Literally and figuratively, there was a funk in there tonight. She should probably stop driving the thing soon. But sometimes, a BMW wasn't the car to take to a strip club when you didn't want to be noticed.

Driving the miles to her club without even registering what she was doing, she looked at the dark city as she went. It looked the same as it had her entire life. During the day, it looked different and unfamiliar, but at night, she could navigate it with ease. She was born into these night streets. Both her mother and grandmother had been hookers, and maybe the generation before, she would never know. Her father was non-existent. There was no way for her mother to pinpoint who it could have been.

The man who chopped cars was only around for around five years, then was gone. The one who sold drugs, maybe a year. Her fun grandpa was just some guy who managed the apartment building. He would give her mom and grandma discounts on the rent for a few hours behind closed doors. There had never been a man who had stuck around, but she'd had never wanted one to either.

Her life at been just that fucked up until she was fourteen. That was the year she got arrested for running a meth lab. If any of the cops had bothered to look at her school record, they would have seen she had no actual knowledge of science. She had missed more school than she had been to for years. Selling the meth, yes, she had done that. That was her job. Making it? Impossible.

But it had been that crime that had landed her in reform school, away from her mom and grandma, who cut all ties to her the day she was arrested. Aurora was sure they had skipped town or at least neighborhoods and started all over again without her. But she had never looked into them. Never. In fact, by the time she had met Winter, she was no longer Heaven Carlyle; she was Aurora. And even if Heaven would've been a great stripper name, she had never used it. That name was her past.

After paying a lawyer for a quick name change when she had two cents to rub together, she was Aurora. Winter Rose Night had always complained about her name, and it was so much worse than just Heaven. *Winter Rose Knight.* To this day, she went by Winnie, which was too cutesy for what Win looked like. Dark and brooding, Win was Win.

Aurora pulled to the back of the parking lot. There was no need to take up a prime customer parking spot. The lot was packed for that time of night, and the sight had her grinning as she pushed open the front door.

The scene that met her was exactly what it should be: a few dozen customers and three girls on stage doing their thing. Nobody noticed her come in. There were three sets of tits on the stage to distract. At the bar, Trish pointed her to the back, where the break room was.

Pushing inside, she saw a stranger sitting on the bench with an icepack pressed to her eye. She looked young and more scared than anything. She was midsized with mousy brown long wavy hair and green eyes not unlike Aurora's. Musing as she looked at the girl, Aurora thought maybe they had the same fucking father out there somewhere. It was the same thing she considered whenever she came across a green-eyed person.

"How did you get the black eye, sweetheart?" Aurora asked.

She had talked to women in trouble many times over the years. But it was something she never got used to. Men could be awful. It never ceased to amaze Aurora what they would do to a woman they claimed to love.

"Can I just leave?" the girl asked, looking right into her eyes in defiance.

Aurora looked over the girl who could probably legally drink, but just barely. Her gut said she wasn't stripper material, not that she hadn't been surprised before, but not often. And she could but money on not today.

"I need to know what happened first."

Aurora sat on the bench across from her. Something had happened, and Aurora was getting to the bottom of it—no matter what the girl wanted.

"It was nothing. I want to leave now." She was now more angry than scared, and she was not breaking eye contact.

"Not until we get this straightened out, Sweetheart." Aurora wasn't exactly happy right now either.

"I want to see the owner." The girl threw the ice pack on the ground, and it skittered across the gray tiles. "I've already asked, and nothing. Now you."

"You have me, girly." Aurora folded her arms across her ample chest. "I'm the owner, Aurora Carlyle."

Her big green eyes widened, and the girl looked her up and down as if she suddenly mattered. Then she stopped for longer than she should have on Aurora's substantial chest.

Aurora snapped her fingers. "Eyes up here girl. What do you want?"

The girl blushed scarlet. "I want a job."

"This isn't the way to apply for a job," Aurora said firmly.

Fights only resulted in getting banned from the property, not in job offers.

"But I want to work here." The girl's eye was already gray around the edges. By morning, it would be purple.

"Honey, you cannot work here."

"I can! There is nothing I can't do," she insisted with a determination Aurora admired in the women she hired, usually.

It was too late at night for this. "What's your name?"

"Gardi West."

"Tell me, that's neither your real name nor a stripper name," Aurora demanded.

Gardi's chin went up. "It's my name."

"Well, Gardi, you're missing some key components to work in a place like this." Aurora looked at her with annoyance.

"What?" the kid asked.

"Tits and an ass. Guys are not all that interested in what you have."

Aurora hated to say it, but it needed to be said. Because she didn't want this kid here at all, this kid didn't belong here.

"So, I can't do it because I don't have some huge rack?" The girl turned an even darker shade of red.

"Yes, and because you're blushing just talking about it. You have to learn to call them what they are, tits."

Aurora wanted the kid to run home to her parents so fast that she never thought about this place again. There were people who needed this job. Who thrived at this job. Gardi's nails were professionally manicured. They were professionally painted in fuck-you-mom-and-dad purple.

"I can show off my tits." Her face beat red as she crossed her arms because Aurora knew she didn't want to.

"Do it. Off with the shirt." Aurora pointed at her soft blue v-neck t-shirt.

Green eyes locked with hers, and the kid blushed more scarlet than Aurora had seen in years. By the time women came here, they were usually pretty comfortable showing off their tits. Aurora actually never asked to see them before hiring strippers. Because no matter what she told this kid, guys would look at any size tits that were visible.

Gardi was biting her bottom lip so hard that Aurora was sure she would draw blood. But the kid was more stubborn than Aurora had bargained for, and she whipped off the shirt and balled it in her hands. Leaving her clad in only a light pink bra.

"Nice tat," Aurora said.

She eyed the tiny star just above the girl's belly button. Just another small example of a kid rebelling against her parents.

"Shut up." The girl hissed.

Aurora laughed at her expression. "The tits are lacking."

The kid was going to die in this room. The girl wasn't going to be able to serve drinks around here if she couldn't take criticism.

"Fuck you." She squeezed the shirt tighter in her hand.

"Nope, you're not my type. And you're no stripper, Gardi West. Go home, and if you really need a job, there is always something at the mall."

Aurora got up. This had taken way too much of her time already. It was the middle of the night, and she was ready to be home.

"I just want to be a waitress," the girl begged, sensing her opportunity was almost over.

"Tell you what." Aurora grabbed the shirt she was still clutching to her chest and said, "If you can walk across the bar right now in just that, I'll hire you."

Not giving her the option, Aurora took the shirt as she walked out of the room. At the bar, she told Trish to cut the music, and the dancers stopped. This wasn't something she'd ever done before, but she wanted this kid back where she belonged. *Immediately.*

Gardi was up to something, and Aurora wanted to see what she was willing to do. Standing next to the bouncer, she watched as the girl peeked out from the back area. Since she was the only thing moving, all eyes turned to her. Even if she wanted to be a waitress, she would have to learn to be looked at and be half-naked as she did.

Even with all eyes on her, she came into full view, her arms down and her pale pink bra showing. As she walked toward Aurora and the bouncer, a few customers made catcalls, and the kid went red from chest to hairline. But she was doing it with a steely determination that Aurora had been convinced the kid would be lacking. *Had hoped she was lacking.*

When she was three feet away, Aurora tossed her shirt back and motioned for the music to continue. Gardi put her shirt on and crossed her arms.

Grinning, she said, "I did it."

"That you did. Tomorrow, at Rising Passions, be there by ten. I'll be there. This club is a little rough for you, kid," Aurora stated none too happily at the kid's success.

She should have had her take her bra off, too. Maybe then she would have failed. But Aurora had never expected her to pass.

"I'll be there." Gardi sounded excited about her good fortune.

"I won't be mad if you don't show," Aurora said and opened the door for her to leave. "You could stay home with your happy family. Ask your dad for some money. He's got enough to share."

The kid's eyes went wide in surprise. "How did you know?"

"Your jeans cost more than my car payment." Aurora pointed to them, and the girl seemed embarrassed about it as she walked away. Staying by the door watching her go, Aurora hoped that she wouldn't ever see her again.

Of course, Gardi got into a fairly new Honda and drove off. What was that kid up too? It had taken everything in her to walk across that bar, but whatever she was doing was worth the humiliation. What could possibly be worth it to her?

CHAPTER
Two

Nick: Got her, will tail her.

DECLAN CHAMBERLAIN finally pushed himself away from the bar, looking around the room as he did. The music was back on, and the dancers were back on stage strutting their stuff. But his mind was more focused on the fact that the woman he knew as Aura had walked into a strip club like she belonged there. The very woman he had spent almost two years trying to forget about.

What was only supposed to be some clean fun after his second divorce had turned into an intense and addicting affair. He wanted to see her every day and was angry and irritated when he didn't. Then she had ended it and was gone. And no amount of detective work had found her, and that was his job, finding people.

Now, here she was in the middle of a strip club in the middle of his latest job. She probably wouldn't recognize him anymore. After their little affair, he had trimmed his long hair and shaved his beard. He'd also started working out nearly every day. In the beginning, it had been just to get her off his mind. Now it was more of a habit.

Gardner Westmoreland had left with her clothes on, at least. What she was even doing in the building, much less walking across it topless, was beyond Declan. The kid was born with a silver spoon in her mouth. Everything she ever wanted was handed to her, mostly before she even asked. Her family was old money in this town, old enough that they acquired their fortune in the old country.

Hell, her name was Gardner. Who gave that name to a kid unless they knew that kid would never be picked on? He was sure that kid had never been picked on. She had never even glimpsed how the other half lived. And she had never been in a strip club until tonight. And he had no idea why she was even there.

He had been only five minutes behind her when she came into the place an hour before. By the time he arrived, she was already in the middle of a fight with the bouncer, the bartender, and two strippers. Gardner Westmoreland had lost, and she had been taken to the back of the place, sequestered in titty bar jail. Declan had expected cops to show up and haul her away, but instead, half an hour later, the leggy blond from his past had shown up. She must be some sort of manager, no longer the stay-at-home mom that she had been before? Or had that been a lie?

In the half an hour he had waited for Gardner to be released from titty bar jail, he had looked around the place. He never thought he would end up here when he and his firm had been hired by Royal Westmoreland to guard his daughter last week. At twenty-three, she was able to spread her wings, but in a safe way. It was up to Declan and a team of six to make sure she was safe while she was away from home. She could do whatever she wanted, just safely.

That meant Declan was babysitting the kid, but at least he had help. Nick would make sure she got home or to another strip club if that was what she wanted to do. If she didn't go home, Declan would get another text about it. But after six days, he was tired of watching her do nothing. Mostly, she stayed home. Declan thought it was going to be a cakewalk. Tonight, it had been completely different.

In the years he had been running his own company, he had never had to just watch a woman and make sure nothing happened to her. Most of the time, there was some danger involved. Someone was trying to hurt someone or kill someone. Blackmail and kidnappings were not out of the possibility. Babysitting wasn't his cup of tea.

Pushing his way out of the bar, he almost ran over the leggy blonde. Grabbing her around the waist, he pulled her closer to prevent her from going flying on impact. Holding her tight to him was not unpleasant. Her breasts were smashed nicely to his chest, and her waist was as dainty as it had looked when she was in the bar. And his body definitely remembered being this close to hers.

Upon impact, her fingers had dug into the shirt he was wearing, and her nails scraped his skin as they clamped on. Her green eyes were bright with surprise, and she was breathing heavily as he lowered her to the ground.

"Sorry, ma'am," he said, taking in her bright green eyes, remembering how they looked when she climaxed. Even after all this time, the memory was still fresh.

Her red lips curled into a half grin. "Ma'am. I like that."

Not able to take his eyes off her lips, he said, "I don't know your name."

Her hands were still holding his shirt, and he was still holding her close, close enough that she could probably tell what he was thinking and feel how her nearness was affecting him.

"Aurora, and yours?"

"Declan," he said before remembering he was supposed to be Kyle today.

Didn't matter, the girl was long gone, and she was not coming back here. If she did, he would stay away.

"Did you see anything you liked tonight, Declan?" Her hand dropped down his shirt only to run down the outsides of his legs as far down as she could reach, then went back up.

"Not until I left."

He'd told her the truth. As his grip on her loosened, his hand slid low to cup her ass. It felt like the past two years hadn't even happened. Here she was in his arms again.

"Sorry to hear that. I'll bring it up in the next employee meeting." Her half grin was back. It made her laugh lines more visible since they were only on one-half of her face.

"Not their fault." He pulled her close to him. He couldn't help it. "I like a little more mystery than they provide."

"I think that you smell of cop, and cops don't like titty bars." Her hands pulled away from his sides and dropped flat to her sides.

"I'm not a cop. I can promise you that." He released her completely, regretting the new space between them. It had been so long since he was a cop that he barely remembered that part of his life.

Backing away from him, she looked him up and down, and Declan hoped she didn't recognize him, or maybe he hoped that she did. He wanted her in his life again.

"If my granny taught me nothing, it was how to smell a cop. You don't pass the sniff test."

"Not a cop," he said. "But I will walk you to your car and make sure nothing happens to you."

"Both the parking lot and the club are safe, Officer Declan." She headed toward the cars in the back of the lot.

"It'll make me feel better to see you safely there." He followed her across the parking lot, not wanting to end his time with her again. He wanted this moment to last as long as he could manage.

"See, that's cop stuff," she pointed out.

"Not a fan of cops, Aurora?" He liked her name. It suited her better than Aura, and he couldn't be mad she had used an alias. He'd done the same.

"Cops are fuckers," she said as if that explained it all.

"All of them?" he questioned. He knew a lot of cops; his dad had been a cop, and most of his past and current friends were cops.

"Show me a good one, and I can show you millions that are fuckers." She turned and looked him up and down. "Are you a good one or a fucker?"

He took the middle ground on her question. "I'm not a cop."

"Do you always try to pick up girls at titty bars, Declan?" Her eyes looked him up and down again.

"First time," he admitted because he was trying to pick her up. "Is it working?"

"No, you're a cop," she denied, but her eyes were saying he was succeeding.

"Liar, you don't care if I'm a cop right now." His hand went around her slim waist and pulled her to him, needing to touch her again.

"Cops are fuckers," she said, less harshly than the last time she said it.

"God, you are hot," he said as his lips found hers.

Despite her words, she responded immediately by slipping her tongue into his mouth and pulling his waist closer to her body, rubbing her core against his erection. It was still as incredible and fiery as it had been before.

His fingers slid under her shirt, and she leaned into his hands as he cupped her breasts through the lacy bra. Declan remembered just what they looked like and felt like and that they were a hundred percent her. But it had been a while since he had actually been with a woman, and it was showing. He couldn't stop touching her warm skin and couldn't get his mind around how to get her damn bra off.

Pulling away from her mouth, he tried to come to his senses. They were in a parking lot at a strip club, and all he wanted to do was have sex with this woman again. It was his only thought. It didn't matter the location, he was just happy they were in a dark corner and not visible to the strip clubs door.

While he was trying to get under control, she unbuttoned his jeans and slid her hand inside. All thought was gone when her fingers slid over his erection, cupping it through his boxers. Groaning, he redoubled his effort to get the damn bra off. He failed again when her hand slid into his boxers and started to stroke him in earnest.

"Nice cock Declan. Would it get harder if I said my car has no insurance?" Her laugh made him groan as she continued to touch him.

"I'm not a cop," he said again as he gave up with the bra, slid his hands down her body, and then pushed up her skirt.

Looping a finger on the top of her panties, he pushed them down her legs so he could touch her wet core. She groaned as his fingers played with her clit until her breath caught, and she moaned.

Feeling her slide a condom on, he had no idea where it had come from but knew what she wanted. Grasping her hips, he lifted her, and she wrapped her legs around his waist. He slid deep into her, groaning at the heady sensations it was causing. This was what he had dreamed of for two fucking years. All he managed was a few vigorous pumps, and it was over. Not the performance that he had played through his mind when he imagined them hooking up again. But it had been perfect since she was there and it wasn't a dream.

Wiggling free of him, she slid to her feet. Straightening her outfit, she said, "You're a pretty good fuck, for a cop."

With that, she pushed him away, walked around the car, and got in. He tried to say something witty, but nothing came out. Would now be a good time to ask for her number? Her last name? It was too late when she shut her door and started the car. As she backed out, she waved at him. Then, with wheels spitting up gravel, she was gone.

Watching her taillights disappear, he remembered that his pants were still open and his penis was hanging out. Shoving it back into his pants, he pulled off the condom and tossed it on the ground. After buttoning his pants, he shook his head and picked it back up to toss it in the garbage by his pickup. Can't litter.

As he drove home, he wondered what the hell had happened. He had never ever done something like that. He didn't even know if her name really was Aurora. Would he be able to find her again? Did she work at the club all the time? What did she do there? He had to concentrate on Gardner.

Not a stripper that had been able to make him forget everything with just a touch. He had even managed to stop thinking about a soccer mom who he had no leads on finding. This time he knew exactly how to find Aurora if he wanted to. He just had to figure out if he wanted to.

Pulling into his driveway, he saw his daughter's car parked in front of the garage. She was supposed to be at the dorms, not here. In the living room, he saw her on the couch, still up, watching TV.

"What are you doing here, Reese?" he yelled.

"Really, you're going to yell at me. My roommate's having sex with her boyfriend at my place, Dad. I needed a place to sleep. You're out all hours of the night, and I get yelled at?" Reese yelled at him.

"Tell her to stop having sex." Declan declared. "I'm an adult. I can stay out as late as I want."

"Next time, I'll just suggest that they stop," she said sarcastically.

Declan could have hugged his daughter for her wit. Nothing got her down. But he probably smelled of sex, so he thought better of it.

Reese was almost twenty-one and wouldn't be afraid to point out the smell if she knew what it was. Reese was going to give the world a run for its money one day. And he was excited to get to see it happen.

"Come over any time you need to. This was the first late night on this case, and I wasn't ready for it," Declan admitted.

"I could help you. I could become her friend, make it easy." Reese was always trying to become a part of his company, but she needed her degree more than anything.

Then they might talk about her being involved then, but probably not. He didn't want his daughter in the business he was in. That is why she was in college and not a cop. He'd lived that life once and wanted better for her.

CHAPTER
Three

"FUCKITY FUCK," Aurora chanted as she drove back uptown to her apartment.

What had she done? Sure, she wanted to get laid, but not in her parking lot with a stranger who was probably a cop. And it was all on tape. She knew the cameras were there the entire time. And Chuck, who was in charge of security, would get a kick out of seeing her come on camera. She had to be up at dawn to get the tape and destroy it. And it was nearly dawn as it was.

Odd as it might sound coming from a former stripper, she was not a bed hopper. Sure, she and Win joked about sex, but she didn't always enjoy it. A hookup now and again was just as good as anything, and she wasn't even looking for a relationship. Though secretly, she wanted Win in one and had pushed quite a bit when she had met Daniel, which had turned out perfectly.

Win was going to laugh her ass off at this, a cop. Neither friend was into cops. Each had been arrested maybe one time to many before reform school. Aurora couldn't even see a traffic cop without turning the other way and bolting. Cops were her secret enemy. The secret was that they didn't know it.

But this cop was so fucking sexy, she couldn't stop looking at him and then touching him. Obviously. If he hadn't had a condom in his pocket, she had no idea what she was going to do. Sure, she picked his pocket, but it wasn't for money. Just because she had gifts didn't mean she always used them for evil. Just getting a condom when needed.

Pulling into Win's parking spot, she jumped out and kicked the tires of the old car and hoped Win didn't notice. Smiling, she knew Win wouldn't suspect a thing. Win didn't notice much unless it was a number. She was one hell of an accountant.

As the elevator took her to the top floor, she tried not to think about smoky gray eyes and silky black hair. Or the sensation of his hands on her skin. *No,* she demanded of herself to think of something else. *Anything else.*

Opening the door to her apartment, she admired her view, as she always did. For years, she and Win had shared a two-bedroom cheapo apartment on the second floor of a rundown building, just saving for the day when they could afford something like this. And that day was here. Walking over to the sliding doors to her balcony, she watched the sun rising in the east. She had never been on her balcony, never. Her apartment was too high for her comfort. She was never going out there. But Win had wanted a place with a balcony, and Aurora could never say no to her friend.

Because *not* saying no to Win had gotten her here. Win had wanted to get a high school diploma, so Aurora got one too. Win had wanted to go to college for business, so Aurora did too. Win had wanted an MBA, so Aurora got one too. Win wanted this place so close to her work that she could walk, so Aurora drove every day to get to her work and paid a premium to be downtown. By saying yes to Win, Aurora had become a successful businesswoman.

Turning her back on the city, she went to take a shower and start her day. By noon, she would be back here and crash for five hours until Millie came home, but before that she had a recording to delete, and an interview with a potential employee. One she really hoped wouldn't show up.

Once dressed for the day in her leather skirt and white blouse, she went across the hallway, this time knocking because it was only six a.m. Win opened the door, already dressed for the day in a light green suit sans matching jacket and heels. But the shoes would be added by the time she walked out the door for the day.

Win walked away once the door was open. "Late night or early morning?"

"Two a.m., which is that?" Aurora asked, seeing Millie was already up and eating in her highchair.

"That is a shit time to go to work." Win brought her over a cup of coffee. "Are you staying home today?"

"Yes, this morning. Do you think Penny will take her the entire day today? I was thinking I would take tomorrow off, maybe keep Xander for her."

Penny was Win's newly minted mother-in-law, and she had been babysitting Millie since she was born. Xander was Win's stepson, who was now six. Sometimes, Aurora almost cried at how accommodating Win and her family were to her. Penny didn't have to watch Millie, and Daniel didn't have to drive her to and from daycare. But they happily did. Penny and her husband had even invited her to holidays, *holidays*!

"She doesn't mind, Rora. She worked when her kids were small. She understands things come up. I'll just have Daniel take her out there this morning with Xander," Win said as her eyes went to the back of the apartment as Daniel himself walked out of the bedroom.

God, that woman loved her Daniel.

"What about me, Fred?" Daniel asked, using the nickname for his wife that made no sense. Her name was Winter, not Winifred. But it was her name on the app they had met on, so he kept using it.

"You're taking Millie this morning with Xander. Rora was up most of the night at one of the clubs. She needs sleep." Win straightened the man's already straight tie as an excuse to touch him.

"Actually, I've to go to the club this morning," Aurora said. "Job interview." She really hoped the girl would bail on it.

"Stripper?" Daniel asked, pouring himself a coffee.

He secretly loved that her employees were strippers, and he didn't so secretly love that his wife had been one once. Not that anyone at the company they worked at knew that fact. Win hated people knowing about her past. Aurora thought she was a better person for what she went through. But convincing Win of that wasn't easy.

"God, no. This kid came in last night, started a fight, and then requested a job from me."

"Showing initiative?" Win asked, already futilely sweeping up the cereal Millie had dropped on the floor. Her best friend hated messes.

"Showing a complete lack of a brain. She's titless, assless, and shy as shit." Aurora knew she was being harsh but was unable to stop herself.

"Why are you hiring her?" Daniel asked. He knew she didn't hire people just to hire people.

"Because I told her if she could walk across the bar topless, she had a job. She did it," Aurora admitted.

She shouldn't have set the bar low enough for the kid to achieve the goal.

"But only a waitress?" Win asked as Xander came walking into the room, still in his cartoon-themed pajamas.

"Morning, Rora," Xander said as he took the chair next to her. He always said hi to her and seemed happy to see her.

She rubbed his head. "Morning, handsome."

This kid thing was getting easier and easier. When Win had hooked up with Daniel, neither she nor Win had ever been around that many kids. Both admitted to puking more often than not when left alone with them, but over the last year, it had just turned into something they were comfortable with. They were both raising kids.

"You should see this kid. Her jeans cost maybe six hundred dollars, and the T-shirt she casually wore into my strip club was from one of those high-end stores you don't find in a mall. Her necklace had a dozen diamonds on it. Real ones. She was slumming for some reason. I'll hire her, and I'll make sure that no one touches her on my property. I just hope she gets it out of her blood quickly."

Aurora put down her empty coffee cup.

"Doesn't sound like fun," Win said, releasing Millie from the high chair before handing her over to Aurora.

Snuggling her daughter, she, for some reason, thought of the guy in the parking lot this morning. The dark hair and gray eyes were a coincidence. She had a type, after all. But there was something about his touch that brought up feelings she had pushed down two years before. She wasn't letting them out either.

Taking Millie back to her apartment, she got the girl ready for the day in a little pink tracksuit and put a pink bow in her thick black hair. Aurora secretly loved dressing up her baby girl, though maybe it wasn't a secret based on the kid's closet. She chalked it up to her crappy childhood.

Win came in as Aurora was putting tiny pink shoes on her daughter's feet. Then she analyzed the chubby-cheeked little girl and kissed her wet lips before hugging her tight. Handing her off to Win, she knew the baby was in good hands but hated that they weren't hers. Daniel would bring the baby home to her tonight, and tonight, she would spend all her time with the little lady.

But now she had a rich waitress to hire. And a security tape to get rid of. Her day was going to be interesting.

THE TEXT CAME in just after nine a.m. that Gardner was on the move. Declan had only had about three hours of sleep. Of course, Aurora had dominated his thoughts before he had fallen asleep, and she dominated them while he slept, and now he had new images to add to the old ones. Everything that had happened between them was stuck on repeat in his mind.

Climbing into his truck, Declan wondered about the girl he was tailing. Hadn't she gotten home too late to be up this early? Declan longed for that kind of energy again.

Backing out of his driveway, he noticed Reese's car was gone. He just hoped she would stay in school this time. He knew she was as bored with her classes as he had been, but he had always wanted her to get a degree. He had once wanted one, but life had gotten in the way and he wasn't going to let that happen with his daughter.

Years ago, when her mom had taken off without looking back, Declan had been nervous about raising a twelve-year-old girl alone. A kid he hadn't spent enough time with before because he was too busy working long hours. Busy being a breadwinner like his dad, a man who hadn't taken much interest in Declan's life.

Looking back he could see it wasn't how he wanted to raise his daughter. She needed someone there for her so he had quit the force to spend more time with her. Starting his own security business was supposed to be better hours with more time to spend with his kid. After a lot of hard work and hiring the right employees, that was true.

For years, he had put everything into the company and had made it a success. Though his relationship with his daughter had improved with his new job, his sex life had suffered. Yes, he had managed to find women to date, but they always got tired of his hours and the time he spent with his daughter. Every time a woman made him choose between his daughter and them, Reese won. Something that wouldn't change even if she was an adult and living on campus Reese was his number one priority.

A few years ago, he had thought that he found a woman who understood, a woman he thought he could grow old with, so he had married her. Within a year he realized that he had made a mistake, she had pretended to want to be a mother. Instead she had treated Reese badly behind his back, and had wanted Declan to send Reese to her mother. Something that would never happen since the woman had no interest in her daughter anymore. When he had said as much to her, she had thrown a tantrum, claiming that he didn't love her. Turned out she was right, any love between them was gone when he found out how she had treated his daughter.

When that marriage ended, he focused all his attention back on his company until he was successful enough to turn down jobs, but guarding the princess was too much money to pass up. Except it was starting to be more work than he had expected. Apparently, the girl couldn't get enough of strip clubs because she had just walked into another one. This time, her head was held higher than the night before. She was showing a confidence in herself he hadn't seen from her in the weeks he had been following her.

Sitting in the car outside a strip club, he waited to tail her when she came back out. Nick was already on the inside, and Declan hoped he had his eyes on Gardner and not the mostly naked women inside. It was a different club than the night before. This one was called Rising Passions. *Cute.*

Pulling out his laptop, he looked up as much information as he could find on it. The owner of record was Aurora Carlyle, his Aurora? Did the woman from last night and all those months ago run her own business? He had seen beyond the soccer mom lie. She was not the sort that would be happy doing nothing all day. But he could see her being successful at anything she tried.

Another search on his computer told him she had no record, not a thing. She apparently drove a BMW, but not last night. The Buick was not listed under her name. Her address was actually downtown, miles from here. Why would she pay the high prices of downtown when homes around the club were larger?

A car door slamming nearby made him look up and see the woman herself walking across the parking lot. Today, she was in a white blouse with a deep V-neck, showing off more cleavage than a banker would wear to work at ten in the morning. She pulled it off, though. She looked great. Her heels were high, and she had no issues walking across the loose gravel in them. Her white-blond hair was piled on her head in a loose, very loose bun. On her shoulder was a bag big enough to carry a computer that matched her skirt's tan leather perfectly.

Watching her ass as she pushed into the door, he was surprised she was here so early. She had to have gotten only as much sleep as he had gotten, but she looked put together and ready for the day. He, on the other hand, hadn't showered and had forgone shaving for a few more minutes of sleep.

Back on his computer, he pulled up her driver's license. She looked the same in person as in the smiling picture, a bland smile, not that gorgeous half smile. Green eyes, blond hair. Her height and weight were lies, but a lot of people lied about that information. She was thirty-seven, which surprised him. But since he was forty-five, she was young to him.

Also, it seemed she was the proud owner of a strip club, one that his latest assignment had been inside for half an hour already.

But what exactly was Gardner doing here? She had money and power at her disposal. He couldn't figure out her motives. Sure, he hadn't been hired to figure out why she was doing what she was doing. But his mind wouldn't let go of the disconnect.

And now the woman he had looked high and low for last year was so near, and he couldn't show his hand, not yet. He had to get to the bottom of all this first. Then, he could focus all his attention on the blonde.

CHAPTER
Five

THE KID SHOWED UP. Aurora knew she would, even though she hoped she wouldn't. Even before Aurora arrived, someone had shown her to Aurora's booth, and the kid was sitting there, all freshly showered in a cashmere sweater and jeans. Leather fashion boots peeked out from under the table like they were meeting at a local hangout to get lunch. Like the mall.

Sliding into the booth, Aurora set her laptop bag on the bench beside her. Taking her time, she pulled out the computer, booted it up, and set it aside as it came to life like so many other days in this place. She had an office in the back, but she never used it, preferring to be among the employees and customers instead. The steady noise kept her focused on her work far better than silence ever did.

Only when she had her 'desk' set up did she turn her attention to the young woman. "So you came."

Perkily, she slid a paper over to Aurora. "Yes."

Aurora studied the application. Gardi West, age twenty-three, even a social security number. It was filled out, but most of it was a lie. Aurora dealt with people every day running from something. This kid was the complete opposite of that, but she was pulling all the same stunts as so many others.

She slid the paper into the bag, having memorized it in the short amount of time it had been in her hands. A photographic memory always came in handy, from memorizing PIN numbers for ATMs as a kid to test-taking in college. Her memory had yet to fail her.

"Why?" she asked as a waitress brought over a bottle of sparkling water and a glass of ice, Aurora's drink of choice.

Sitting up straighter, Gardi stated, "I need a job."

"Bullshit." Aurora leaned back in the booth.

Gardi flinched at Aurora's words. "I do, really."

"Your outfit costs more money than you'll make in a week here. Maybe two weeks. And we aren't even talking about those earrings, diamonds and gold. I wouldn't wear those here again. For some people, that kind of money is the difference between scraping by and getting ahead," Aurora told her, wishing the kid would just leave. She didn't belong here.

Gardi touched her ears for a moment and lied, "They aren't real. I need this job so bad."

"I'm going to let you have your dream, kid. You can be a waitress for as long as you like. But you won't be going on stage, and if you cause any trouble, you're out. Three days a week and days, no nights. There is no way you can be trusted during the night. That's when the real customers come here." Aurora wrote everything in shorthand in a notebook she always carried with her. She had fallen in love with the quick writing style during her college days.

"Why not on the stage? Are my breasts really that small?" She looked down at them like a kid would.

"Yes, and you just called them breasts. And also, you don't have the personality to be on stage. It takes more than want to be successful up there. It takes desire. Wednesday nights at six is a pole dancing class, and I would suggest you be here for that. That's unpaid, but for you, mandatory." She added another note on the paper.

"Okay," the girl said with more delight than the job offer warranted. Like it was her dream job.

"Talk to Trish at the bar, and she will give you the uniform. Invest in a pushup bra and good shoes," Aurora suggested. Her no-sleep night was starting to get to her because the kid's excitement was rubbing off on her.

"Thank you, Aurora. I won't disappoint you." The kid actually clapped her hands in excitement. Because it seemed she was unable to contain it. *At all.*

"Start next Wednesday. Then be ready for class." Aurora had to remember to tell everyone to keep an eye on her. Gardi had no idea how to handle men.

Making a mental note to add her to the schedule later today, she slipped the notebook into her bag. She wanted the girl to leave, but she just sat there. Sat there looking at her. Like they weren't done with the interview.

"Do you go to the class?" Gardi asked.

"Yes, usually."

Aurora had actually dragged Win with her to class. Daniel would watched the kids that night. He seemed to realize early that she and Win needed time alone together. Pole dance class was their time. Or he wanted his wife to pole dance. Either could be the reason.

"Do I need special clothes?" Gardi questioned.

"Don't wear anything that costs more than fifty dollars," Aurora suggested. "These women are not as rich as you."

"I'm not rich," the kid said with a straight face as she crossed her arms over a four-hundred-dollar sweater.

"I didn't assume you were, but your parents are, sweetheart. You're on the schedule for Wednesday. Show up if you want. If you don't, I won't be upset."

Slipping her computer back into her bag, Aurora slid out of the booth. She wasn't going to sit there all day. She had a nap calling her name.

As she pushed out the door, she saw Gardi at the bar looking at the shirt she was going to wear. The kid had no idea how much of her body the shirt actually revealed. Wednesday was going to be very interesting.

Tossing her bag in the backseat, Aurora climbed into the front seat, but she had a feeling she was being watched. Not by the cameras in the parking lot, either. She was used to those. Looking around her, she saw nothing amiss in the parking lot, but her sixth sense was telling her a different story. One more sweep of the parking lot revealed nothing.

Before she got the engine started, the kid rushed out of the club and got into a midsized Ford. A different vehicle than she had been driving the night before. Who was this kid?

After her nap, Aurora would run the social security number. She didn't think Gardi was underage, but she had been surprised before on that front. Her clubs didn't employ underage workers or sell sex. Those were her two hard and fast rules since those would send you to jail the quickest. There was no way Aurora was ever going to jail. She had worked hard her entire adult life to stay out of jail.

There was no way she would survive behind bars. She wasn't made for that life. Even if she had been born into a life that should have sent her there, she'd gotten out.

CHAPTER
Six

FOR A GOOD MONTH NOW, Gardner Westmoreland, the oldest daughter of the town's richest billionaire, had been working at a strip club three days a week. A schedule that left her just enough time to get a part-time job with an ambulance-chasing lawyer uptown on her off days. She was really slumming with two jobs, but it was keeping her busy. It had taken time to get her schedules straight, but now her work was predictable, which was nice for Declan and his team.

Four days a week, she worked until noon at the law office. Then, she did a five-hour shift from one to six at the strip club. On Wednesday, she stayed late and took some kind of class in the evening, and on Saturday, she worked the day shift. So far, Declan hadn't needed to go inside any of her places of employment.

Sitting outside the law office was boring, and he usually had someone on his team take the mornings. Everyone complained, but not too loudly when he was around. Not that he would change it. He was the boss, so he could choose his shifts.

Instead, he'd taken the afternoon or evening shift at the strip club. Every time the princess and Aurora came out of the building, Aurora looked around as though she could sense she was being watched. She was a cunning one.

It had taken him longer than he would like to admit to realize she had pickpocketed the condom from his wallet. Nothing else. Not a dollar of the cash he had in there or any of his credit cards. Just the condom that had been in there for far too long but was suddenly gone.

So far in the last month, he'd had to reassign two of his employees, good ones too, he'd once thought. One had been kicked out of the club for staring, and the other had gotten too handsy with the waitresses. Declan had out-and-out fired that one. But now he was running low on guys for the club. Two were starting to get noticed, and that left only him since the new guy wasn't completely trained yet.

When Gardi had first been hired at the strip club, he thought watching her and staying out of sight was going to be easy. Except the eyes in that place were aware. Everybody working was watching out for Gardner. They made sure she got decent guys at her tables and removed anyone who tried anything. The bouncer even walked her to her car if nobody else was leaving at the same time.

So far, he had been able to avoid Aurora, but he was going to have to go inside. It wasn't fair to his guys that he wasn't pulling his weight. Not that the guys were complaining about spending their days looking at tits, but they weren't making enough money on this job to afford the drinks and tips they were spending daily.

Aurora had advertised last week for a bouncer. He was going to try and get hired on, but that would mean putting in hours when Gardner wasn't even there. But it would also mean seeing more of the leggy blonde that he was still wasting quite a bit of time thinking about.

As it was, he saw her nearly every day Gardner worked at some point. Whether she was there because of Gardner or because she was always there, she spent most days in the building. On Wednesday, she came for the class that Gardner was taking, bringing her dark-haired friend with her. They would giggle or talk as they went inside and argue as they came back out two hours later. It seemed her friend didn't enjoy the classes, even though she showed up every week.

It was another Wednesday, and Gardner had arrived at her usual one p.m., which was followed soon by Aurora closer to two in her red SUV. It was the highlight of his day to see what little number she wore. She always wore something tight and low cut but always made it classy. Today, she was actually in skin-tight blue jeans and some kind of long-sleeve shirt; it seemed fall was in the air, and she was dressing for the season.

Though he knew Gardner would never come out of the club until after the class this evening, he still was there, just in case. As he watched the building, a silver SUV pulled into the lot and parked right by the door. When the door of the SUV swung open, a familiar dark-haired girl jumped out, grabbed her purse, and was in the door before Declan could get his own door open.

Grabbing his cell phone, he called Nick, his man on the inside today.

Nick answered quickly, "Hey, boss."

"Did my daughter just saunter into that strip club?" Declan hissed. She was twenty and still underage. She couldn't serve or be served alcohol for another month.

After a moment, the man said, "Yes, she did. She's working here based on the shirt she's wearing."

"This is getting out of hand. This kid is fucking off her rocker," he grumbled with no idea which of them he was talking about, Gardner Westmoreland or his own kid.

Reese wasn't slumming it in the club; she was skipping school to be in the club. What was she thinking going in there? What was she trying to prove?

Declan called his baby girl's cell phone, and she didn't answer, which was no surprise. Though he left a lengthy message anyway. Then he called again and left another one.

Suddenly, all he wanted to do was be in that club. It didn't matter if Aurora recognized him. Reese needed to get her butt kicked out of the club if he had to do it himself.

CHAPTER
Seven

AURORA WAS ENGROSSED in the paperwork for her new employee, except nothing was going right. She typed the information into the boxes again, and she got the same error message. The social security number wasn't working. One more time, and she got the same message. The social and the name weren't a match. She scanned the club until she saw Reese Kathleen Nicholas handing a beer to a guy near the stage. She looked so normal. Too normal to work here.

Looking at the information in front of her again, Aurora could pinpoint the boxes that were lies now that she knew there were issues. The name was wrong, the age was wrong, and the social was wrong. Even the job history was most likely a lie. Tomorrow morning, when she was home with Millie, she would call them and see what they had to say. Usually Aurora didn't call references, but she did if someone lied on their app. Sometimes there was a good reason. Reese's were probably not good enough to keep her job.

Until she got this all figured out, she was stuck with two employees that she would have to watch. And so did everyone in the place. Putting them on the same schedule would be easier, and since together they equaled one good waitress, it was a no-brainer.

"Aurora, this guy wants to apply for the bouncer job," Trish said from beside her table.

Aurora had been so engrossed in her work that she hadn't noticed them come up to her. Trish had been with the club since forever and was a great manager. One that Aurora usually didn't micromanage. But with Gardi working, Aurora liked to be in the club when she worked. And now Reese, too. Aurora knew her time at the club would be increasing again. Her other clubs would be neglected until she figured it out.

"Thanks, Trish." Smiling at her employee, she then looked at the prospective employee.

At this point in her career, she still did all the hiring. She only trusted people she had talked with. If it didn't feel right, they weren't hired. Unless it seemed as if they were hiding something, then everyone was welcome lately.

Her heart slammed to a stop as she looked into the gray eyes of Declan, if that was even his real name, from the parking lot. *Fuck.* He was grinning at her because he knew who she was, and she knew who he was. And they both knew what had happened in that parking lot. A month wasn't long enough to forget how hot it had been.

Without her asking, he slipped onto the bench across from her and tossed his application in her direction. Picking it up, she didn't even look at it. Just held his intense gaze.

"I don't hire cops." Laying his application on the table, she smoothed it down with both her hands.

"I'm not a cop." He was still grinning at her as his eyes dipped down to her chest.

Wanting to feel disgusted by the action, she hated that all she felt was longing for his touch. Touched by the hands that were resting on the table too close to hers, close enough to touch. Memories of those hands on her body engulfed her.

"You smell of cop." Tearing her gaze from his hands, she glanced down at the application to read his name, Declan Vincent,

"What does a cop smell like?" He leaned back in the booth, obviously liking her discomfort.

Leaning over the table, she pretended to take a large sniff of him, ignoring the spicy, musky smell that made her tingle in places that shouldn't tingle in her club. "Just like you."

"Why wouldn't you want a cop at your door?"

She waved her hand around her. "Because everyone in here hates cops."

"Because you're into criminal activity, Aurora?" he asked, no grin anymore. He was testing her. Fucking cops.

"You can look all you want, copper. You will find nothing. Squeaky fucking clean." She folded her arms over her chest, blocking his view if he wanted to look again. They were not for him anymore.

As they stared each other down, Declan snagged a waitress, one of the new ones, by the arm. Aurora kicked him hard in the shin under the table. "You don't touch anyone in here. Ever."

"Just getting a drink." With a cocky grin, he didn't acknowledge that she had kicked him. Hard. Though he let go of the waitress.

Turning to her, he said, "Whiskey and coke."

The waitress stood there, looking at Aurora for direction. Nodding in approval at her, Aurora watched her rush away to the bar. She was impressed that the girl remembered on the first day that there was no alcohol allowed at Aurora's table. Since taking over the club she had the rule, it helped to stop the customers from buying her drinks and it stopped the constant temptation to drink again. That included anyone who was sitting with her.

"If you want to work, you better remember that you're never ever to touch anyone in here except the guys you're throwing out. The girls are off-limits twenty-four-seven. If you're here to get fucked by a stripper, go somewhere else," she said as Reese, not her name, set a glass in front of him and left without looking at either of them.

"I don't want to sleep with strippers," he argued, though he looked guilty, which she took as lying.

"I'd like to point out that that is exactly what happened last month," she said quietly, not wanting anyone to hear what she said.

"But I didn't have sex with a stripper that night, did I?" He toasted her and took a drink of the alcohol-free beverage, not showing any signs that he hadn't ordered it that way.

"Fuck you," she hissed, hoping he didn't notice she was blushing in a strip club.

"I already did that, Aurora."

"I hope you have it memorized because it isn't going to happen again."

Setting down his glass, he leaned back in the booth again. "I think about it all the time."

"At least one of us does."

He chuckled. "And there you go, lying to me."

"This isn't the way to talk to me if you want a job," Aurora pointed out as she took a drink of her water.

"I already have the job, Aurora, because you want me here," he said.

"I. Do. Not," Aurora stated, choking on the water in her mouth.

Ignoring her, he looked around the room. "When should I start? Now?"

"Never," Aurora said because he was acting like a cop.

"But you want to see my ass every time you come in here. Or more?" He waggled an eyebrow at her.

"I don't hire cops." She went back to that. Because even if she'd had sex with him, that wasn't really a deal breaker for hiring him, not that she had ever had this happen before.

He pointed to his application. "Not a cop."

She looked down at it and read through his job history quickly. According to the paper, he had spent years being a bartender or bouncer. Looking at him again, she knew it was a lie. His watch screamed that he had money to blow on real leather. In another life, she would have lifted that watch within minutes of him sitting down.

"Why do you want this job?"

"I was let go at my last job, and I really need something else. Would you give me a chance?" he asked, all innocent. Not that he was innocent at all.

"One week, if you piss me off, you're out." She waved at the bar with her empty glass. "And touch a girl again, and you will be out."

He smiled at her. "You won't regret it."

"I already do," she said, looking at his gorgeous smile.

"When do I start?"

"You said today. Trish can get you a shirt, no blue jeans tomorrow, black only." She dismissed him with a flick of her hand.

"Thanks," he said, actually looking relieved as he stood.

"Oh, and Declan, if I ever see a gun on you again, I'll kick your ass out of here myself." She tapped his back, feeling the gun she had been sure he was carrying the entire time. No guns at her place, ever.

Watching him walk away, his stink of cop followed him. Her club was suddenly full of people who didn't belong there. And she just kept hiring them. She was an idiot.

An idiot who was smart enough to know that this all had started when Gardi West had walked into her club. A smart woman would fire the lot of them and get back to business as usual. But her curiosity wouldn't let her...not yet.

HOW THE HELL had she known he had a gun?

Could she smell that, too?

As deep as he had looked into her past, he had found nothing that raised any flags. College and grad school had surprised the shit out of him, though in retrospect, it shouldn't have. She'd a brain hidden in that blond head. She had recently bought the club they had been at that first night but had sold a different one since then. When they'd hooked up the first time, she had four clubs. She was buying and selling clubs left and right.

The only thing that hinted at anything about her dislike of cops was that she graduated from a local reform school. But the only records he could access from there were academic, she was an honor student all three years. But what had gotten her sent to a reform school was sealed because she was a minor at the time.

After talking to Trish, he changed into the required t-shirt and stowed his other shirt and gun in his truck. Though he hated to be without the weapon, there was little to no danger that required a gun in the club. His job was just to keep customers away from Gardner and now Reese.

Now that he was on the inside he should make her quit. There was no reason for two of them to be there. He knew she was trying her hardest to prove to him she could handle the job, but he still wasn't going to hire her after this. She was putting herself in danger and if something happened when she was around he would be forced to choose between her and the client. He didn't want to have to make those kinds of decisions.

The bouncer, Judd, was to train him in today. As he watched the two young women deliver drinks and food to the tables in smaller outfits than either girl should ever wear, he listened to everything about the club that the man knew. It was way more than the public records would have told him.

He was reminded not to touch the girls, and his job was to make sure no one did. Their second job was to make sure the drunks didn't do something they would regret. Judd made sure to emphasize that he wouldn't get away with doing anything stupid in or out of the club. There were cameras everywhere. As he pointed them out, Declan couldn't *not* see them. He would bet that there were some at the other club also. Which only made him grin.

As Declan watched the blonde typing on her computer, Judd pointed out the two young women they had to pay extra attention to. Declan listened to the instructions without giving any indication he knew the women. They were different from the other girls. Judd didn't say how, just different. They could never let anyone who was close to drunk near them, and if they left alone, you had to go with them and make sure they got off the property without an issue. All orders from the top. The top being Aurora Carlyle herself.

By the time Declan had been introduced to most of the other staff, he knew that Aurora was respected by all her employees. Judd couldn't say enough good things about her. Nor could the bartender or the manager. She was understanding and friendly. And it seemed she usually knew what was going on before anyone else.

The thing that surprised him was that she didn't drink, ever. There were no drinks allowed at her table. Her guests didn't drink at the table. People didn't drop off drinks. If someone happened to buy her a drink and send it over, it was always rejected.

Since she owned more than this club, she was usually only here on

Monday, Wednesday, and Friday. Only during the day, mostly in the afternoon. She had managers for her clubs and let them do their jobs. Most of the time.

Over the past month, while surveying Gardner, he had gotten to know her Wednesday pattern down, so when she left at three, he was shocked. She usually left at five, was gone an hour, and was back. Today, she had left early, taking her computer with her.

He wished he was in his truck so he could watch her walk across the parking lot and get into her car. But he would have to settle for her walking by him in blue jeans that hugged her round hips instead. Which was almost as good, until she was gone, and he had nothing to do but his job.

By six, Declan had seen enough tits to last for years. And his kid and his client were the worst, not that they were hanging out, but far too close to it. At five, Reese and Gardner were done with work, had changed into workout clothes, and sat in a booth in the back talking. About what, Declan had no idea; besides being close to the same age, they had nothing in common. But maybe they were bonding over their shitty job like other young kids.

Reese had avoided getting close to him all day, mostly staying across the room from him. But he knew where she lived, so she wouldn't be able to avoid him forever. And she was going to be grounded until he was dead.

Just when Declan had decided that Aurora was not coming back, she bounded into the club as if she owned it, which she did. Her jeans had been exchanged for tight purple spandex that went to her ankles along with a matching top that showed off most of her tits and her flat stomach. The tits he had wanted to see all day. None of the others were this spectacular.

Following behind her was the black-haired woman who wore leggings and an oversized sweatshirt, the same as every week. Both headed straight to the back of the club, each leaving behind a bag in Aurora's booth because that's what it was: nobody else sat there. Not even when she was gone. The younger women headed back when Aurora and her friend did.

Within fifteen minutes, her friend emerged from the back room, yelling something as she stomped out. With a huff, she sat at Aurora's table, opened the bag, and pulled out paperwork and a laptop. To his shock, she started working on something in the back of a titty bar. A drink was dropped off, and she worked for the next hour.

Most of the staff stopped and talked to her at some point as she worked, from the dancers to the waitresses. Even Judd went over and said hi for a moment.

"Who is that?" he asked when Judd came back.

"Win. Aurora's friend. She comes in every week for class. But she hates it." Judd smiled at the admission.

"Why does she come then?" Declan could tell she truly hated it by her sullen expression when she showed up every week, but not the bar. She seemed to enjoy everything about the actual bar and the people in it.

"I think she feels guilty because she got married and can't spend as much time with Aurora as she used to. She used to be in here more," Judd said, looking over the crowd in the room.

"Is she a stripper?" Declan couldn't help but see she had the body for it.

"Win? No way, man. She's some sort of accountant. They've been friends forever," Judd said.

"Is she working?" Declan asked though he knew she was. It was so obvious.

"Oh, yeah, she does most weeks while Aurora does the class. You should see when they both work, they fight over table space like little kids. It always ends in swearing, just like kids." Judd chuckled before frowning and heading toward the stage, where a man was standing too close.

Just then, Aurora walked out from the back of the bar and slid into her booth, but her friend didn't look away from her computer. Aurora looked at her friend working for a second, then slammed the computer in front of her closed. She was rewarded with a double middle finger salute. Then Win started to put her work into piles and load them into her bag.

Judd returned and started to tell him what he needed to watch for now that the place was getting busier. Thus taking his attention from the only person he had eyes for in this place.

When Reese and Gardner walked out of the back room, Judd told Declan he should walk them to their cars. To get used to it. Neither woman acknowledged him as he walked behind them. Today, Gardner was driving her Civic again, and Reese was in her Jeep. He tried to get his daughter alone, but she was on to him and almost ran to her Jeep to avoid him. She was successful and kicked up dirt as she peeled out of the lot.

Gardner was a little more relaxed about it. She even said goodnight to him. He wished her goodnight and then watched her car pull out of the parking lot. Pausing, he waited for his employee, Nick, to follow her out of the lot. Nick would follow her home.

What was she really doing here?

FORCING herself not to look at Declan by the door, Aurora slid into her booth across from Winter. Her friend was, of course, working on something. Most likely for the club, but that didn't matter. This was their time. Pushing the computer shut, Aurora was rewarded with a shot of angry Winter. She was cute mad, which was why Aurora sometimes just pissed her off.

"Bitch," Win hissed as she said, "fuck you" with her hands.

"I'll take it, witch of the night." Aurora reminded her friend of her husband's cute nickname for her when he still hated her guts.

"Looks like you didn't make the full class, either," Win pointed out as she stacked her papers.

Win usually lasted twelve minutes. You could set a timer to the moment she would swear and stop whatever she was doing and leave the room. It didn't matter if she was stretching or actually on the pole. She walked out at twelve minutes every week.

"Close, next week," Aurora said the same thing she always said.

The truth was that her time was over. She couldn't pole dance for two hours anymore, or even one. That baby took a lot out of her.

Gathering up the papers, Win stuffed them back in her bag. "Keep telling yourself that, Rora."

Aurora grinned at her oldest friend. She loved spending time with her. Even with their differences, they still had a shared past that tied them together. Who else could she call at one a.m. when she needed someone to talk to or drag to strip clubs all over the country just to see what she needed to stay competitive? The only person that came to mind was Win.

"Are you knocked up yet?" Aurora asked as her water was dropped off by the waitress.

"Really? That's what you're going to ask me?" Win said, taking a drink of her pop.

Aurora looked her in the eye. It wasn't that she would notice Win wasn't drinking alcohol because, like her, Win was a recovering alcoholic. Well, maybe they were actually both past recovering; it had been over twenty years now. Both had been dry since they were fifteen. But before that, they were both very wet.

"Yes," Aurora said. "That's what I'm asking. It's been three months since that fancy wedding."

Aurora laughed; it was at Daniel's parent's house, which was fancy, but it was a small and quiet affair. The only thing Aurora hadn't liked about it was that Win's parents had been there. She could have done without those people around, which was how they had been for most of Win's life.

Win sniffed. "I'm not ready for another kid."

Win had barely been ready for her ready-made family.

Aurora laughed. "Yes, you are. I see you with Millie. You want a baby."

"They make me puke," Win pointed out, reminding Aurora what happened the first time Win met her now step-son. Back then Win had been convinced she shouldn't be around kids, something her father had told her years before, so when she met Xander she had panicked and been sick. But the more time she spent with him, the better she got. Not since that first meeting had she been actually physically ill.

"Not in a long time. Unless you're knocked up, then they make you puke." Aurora grinned since she had been sick for much of her pregnancy.

"I'm not pregnant," Win stated firmly.

"Yet!" Aurora flicked water at her from her glass.

"I've got to stop coming here with you." Win laughed and looked around. It was busy tonight. Not the way it usually was on a Wednesday. "What's with the lightweights in class tonight? Another titless waitress."

"I'm collecting them now, like Star Wars toys," Aurora admitted. Win would see through her lie if she told one, so she didn't.

"Two does not a collection make," Winter pointed out in her best Yoda voice.

"I got a bouncer who is a cop. A cop." She tried not to look his way…but did. She was fucking weak.

"Why did you hire a cop?" Win leaned back in her booth with a grin and a glance at the door where Aurora had just been looking.

"Fuck if I know. He told me to." She leaned back in the booth also.

"You want to fuck him?" Win asked with one eyebrow raised under her glasses.

"I already did. But that isn't why I hired him. Something is up around here, and I can't figure it out. So, I let them all come in. I'll solve it soon."

Win sat up, fully interested in the conversation. "Wait, when did you fuck him? Today?"

"No, a month ago. It was a mistake, and we all know that," Aurora stated.

"Do we all know?" Win questioned.

"Fuck you, Winter," Aurora barked.

"Fuck you, Aurora," Win shot back with a fucking grin.

"What exactly is this Rosewood Academy?" Aurora stated, ending the conversation about the cop and fucking.

"Why? That's where Xander goes to school."

"Penny gave me a brochure today when I picked up the kids. She said I have to apply now before it becomes impossible."

Aurora liked picking up the kids from a mansion. Win's in-laws were loaded.

"It would be nice to have the kids in the same school," Win pointed out.

"Hey, CFO married to the marketing manager, I don't make enough money for anywhere called Rosewood Academy," Aurora reminded her.

"It'll be cuter when they get married if they attend the same school."

"They will get married, but they won't be attending the same school," Aurora stated.

They talked about this mythical wedding more than they really should. The kids were six and one and would probably grow up closer than siblings. But for now, they could pretend.

"You have money saved. Dip into that," Win told her.

"That is all the money I have. Once I sell the other place, I'll only have this one, and that is just north of daily living money." Aurora spun the water in her glass.

"We should probably buy houses near the school." Win was grinning. "So they can walk to school."

"I can't afford that. Maybe you two should buy your mansion, and I can live above the garage."

Aurora set the glass down. Her friends had become a couple and, as a couple, should live in the burbs.

"I'm not ready to drive to work yet, so you have some time." Win loved living two blocks from her job.

When she and Daniel married, Aurora had been sure the couple would move. After all, their apartment was a two-bedroom. But Win wouldn't hear of it, and they stayed. But Aurora knew it wouldn't be forever. It was just a matter of time.

"Good, I love my place," Aurora said.

"Should we head home?" Win asked but was already getting out of the booth.

"Yeah, maybe I'll get to see Millie before she goes to sleep." Aurora smiled at the thought. There would be no fancy school for her baby because her mom wanted to spend time with her instead of working.

"So, which one did you have sex with?" Win asked close enough to Declan for him to hear because Win knew Judd was married and knew Aurora's lines in the sand.

"Fuck you, Winter," was all she answered, and then looked into the gray eyes that winked at her as she walked past him as they left the building.

Winter was still laughing when they climbed into Aurora's red SUV. Win didn't drive. Aurora hadn't seen her drive but a handful of times in ten years. Driving was Aurora's freedom. The road was hers and hers alone.

Pulling out of the parking lot, Win apologized for embarrassing Aurora in front of the bouncer. It was not accepted, and she wouldn't be forgiven. Not yet, anyway.

There was silence in the car for a while before Win said, "Daniel and I are going on a trip in two weeks."

"Didn't you just have a honeymoon? Key West? Are you going back because you didn't get knocked up?"

Aurora was not going to let up until Win admitted she was knocked up. Nothing got past Aurora Carlyle. At least that was one mystery she had already solved.

"Shut up, no. We are going to visit my father," Win said carefully.

"Oh," was all Aurora could say.

Win's family had disowned her when she was a drug-addicted fifteen-year-old and had only recently reconnected, and that was a very loose connection. Aurora didn't approve of her relationship with them. Not that Win didn't deserve to have her family in her life or that Win didn't need them there. But because they had abandoned her best friend when she needed them the most. And the one time she reached out to them to tell them she'd graduated from high school, top in the class no less, they'd rejected her again. It was Aurora who had found her in the bathroom, nearly dead from slitting her wrists—because of them. There would be no forgiveness from Aurora for them, ever.

"They came to the wedding, Rora," Win pointed out.

"I didn't want them there," Aurora reminded her.

"I've worked to get over it," Win pointed out.

She had actually started therapy after she and Daniel got together. It was Daniel's suggestion, and Win had actually agreed to it. Aurora knew it was helping her. And this felt like something a therapist would make her do. Aurora knew it wouldn't help. The scars were too deep.

"I was there, Winter Rose. They weren't. I thought you were dead.

They didn't care." Aurora tried not to cry at the memory. It was still one of the worst days of her life.

"They have apologized," Win pointed out.

"Not to me," Aurora stated.

"Because you wouldn't talk to them."

"Because they treated you like garbage, threw you away, and now they want you back because you made something of yourself," Aurora said the words because she knew it was what Win was thinking. That maybe they were only interested in her now that she was a success, that if she wasn't who she had become, they would still not want her.

"Maybe they would have wanted me back earlier," Win stated coolly.

"Then they should have put forth the fucking effort, Winter. You were quite findable this entire time. The only thing you ever did was drop his last name, and you only did that because Knight was on your birth certificate. He never even made an effort to change that in the fifteen years he was raising you."

Aurora pulled into the underground parking garage and weaved though it until she got to her spot.

"Because you're so fucking unfindable Aurora? Did you change your name so your family couldn't find you?" Win's temper came back as she flung open her door.

"Yes, I fucking did, Winter. Even before you fucking got there." Following her to the elevator, they both waited for the doors to open.

"Bullshit! Aurora Carlyle."

"You have no fucking clue about what happened to me before you got there, Winter. I was there a year before you even showed up."

She regretted saying it immediately. It was something she had never told her friend, something she had never planned on telling her. Because who she was before was not a part of who she was now.

"Tell me, Aurora. Tell me what fucking happened, then," Win demanded in anger as she poked the elevator button for the twenty-fifth floor.

"No, that past is the fucking past." Aurora was not *ever* going to talk about it.

"What was your fucking name then?" Win asked as the elevator doors opened, and they walked out onto their floor.

"It doesn't matter, Winter!" she yelled at her best friend.

"Fight much in the hallway, ladies?" Daniel was standing at their open door, holding Millie. She was in a new outfit, which meant that something had gone wrong during the course of the day. But it usually did with her daughter.

"Your wife is going to visit her father. I assume you already know." Aurora took the baby from his arms.

"I've heard of the plans," Daniel said, pulling his wife into a hug and kissing her head.

Before Aurora's eyes, her friend's tension evaporated in her husband's arms. It had happened many times before, but it was still an amazing sight. It was the reason she wanted Daniel in her friend's life. He was her everything. Her actual family was usually the reason for the tension.

"I'm really trying not to swear around her anymore, and you're making that nearly impossible, Winter." Aurora turned to unlock the door to her apartment.

"You're doing very well, Aurora," Daniel said. She couldn't tell if he meant it or not.

"I can still use my hands, Daniel." She flipped him off and shut her door behind her.

Leaning against the door, she hugged her baby tight to her. Maybe she was mad because Win was willing to accept the very people who rejected her back into her life. Aurora was going to lose her only family to the family who didn't deserve her. On top of that, Winter could take her family and move away from Aurora. The home Win and Daniel would want was never going to be across the hallway from the home Aurora would be living in. Slowly, since Millie had been born, she had cut back on her income potential.

But Millie was her everything now. Millie deserved her time more than anything she could buy the girl. To have a daughter who knew that she was loved and cherished was more than Aurora had ever received when she was young.

Setting the baby on the floor to play with her toys, Aurora changed into her pajamas and sat down on the couch to watch her. Her little ponytail on the top of her head was long gone, and so were her shoes. Contently, she played alone with the pile of toys.

Did her mom ever watch her play in the evening? Aurora couldn't remember her mom even feeding her in the evening. That was her grandma or the neighbor lady or nobody. How many nights was nobody at home with her?

What was Aurora going to do when Win moved, and she wasn't across the hallway? What would happen when she got a late-night call? Would she take Millie with her? To break up fights or talk to cops? What about Penny? Would she still watch Millie if Daniel wasn't dropping her off or picking her up? What about if Win really did have a baby? Would Penny watch two babies?

And what if that man rejected her friend again? What if he said something, and Win was sent spiraling again? Would Daniel catch her before she fell if Aurora wasn't around? Daniel wasn't there when it happened before.

Trying to get her mind off everything swirling in her head, she slid off the couch to play with her favorite little person. Hugging her little body, Aurora knew that whatever happened with her life, she would always have Millie. Millie would be enough for her. She didn't need anyone else.

CHAPTER

Ten

IT WAS ALMOST eleven in the evening, and Reese had been avoiding Declan's calls for hours. But no way was she getting away with poking her nose into his case. He had enough to worry about without his daughter in the middle of it.

Which was why he had stopped calling and had instead gone for an in-person talk with her. No way could she avoid him if he was in her dorm, which was how he found himself pounding on Room 252 as loud as possible.

He had been surprised at how easily he had gotten into the building. A studious young man had happily held the door open for him, making him wonder why the front door was locked if they let anyone in. Not that he was complaining tonight. Tonight he needed to talk to his daughter and he knew she would never let him into the building willingly.

Before he could pound again, the door opened, and a girl with wild red curls poked her head out, asking in annoyance, "Can I help you?"

"Where's Reese?" he demanded loudly, and she winced.

Her head went back in, and there were whispers. Declan couldn't decide if it was Reese she was talking to or the guy she had sex with all the time. It didn't matter as he pushed the door in. The redhead was so surprised that she let go of the door the moment it moved. Maybe it was time to find his daughter a stronger roommate…who had less sex.

"Reese Chamberlain, what are you thinking?"

His eyes were on his daughter, who was in sweatpants and a more appropriate t-shirt now. No evidence she had boobs at all. It was nice for a father to see.

She got up from her bed, already yelling, "I was getting close to the client. And I did it!"

"Now I have to put in man-hours watching you. I'm already stretched thin," he yelled back as the redhead left the room.

"I'm on the inside now, Dad. I'm on her same shift. You can drop the guys watching her. Save yourself some man power."

Reese didn't back down, but her roommate shot out the door without looking back. So much for any back up from her. Just like always, she had to fight her own battles.

"I need someone in there. What are you going to do if some guy pulls something on her?" Declan demanded.

"I don't know, Dad. I just took karate for twelve years. Or maybe I can just call my fucking dad. He works there now."

"Are you skipping school for this?

"One day a week, and I have only one class that day. The rest I was free for. I was just going to drop that class anyway, math. I can pick it up next semester." She crossed her arms.

He couldn't help but admire her for her take-charge attitude. Only his daughter would worm her way into a case like this.

As if admitting defeat, he told her, "There's no way I'm paying you."

"You think I care? If I prove myself on this one, you will pay dearly for the next one." She couldn't suppress her grin. She knew she had won.

"If you don't mess this one up."

"Me mess it up? That's rich dad." Reese rolled her eyes far more dramatically than she needed to. "She pegged you for a cop the second she saw you."

"Gardner?" he questioned. He had assumed she hadn't even noticed.

"Aurora, Dad, the boss. And Rex is about out. Aurora put him on the watch list today. Better make him scarce," Reese said.

"Why wasn't I told?" He was security.

"Because he doesn't touch your tits, Dad." She touched them herself as if he had no idea what they were.

Slamming his eyes shut, he turned from her. "Don't call them that."

"Bosoms then," she said less dramatically.

"Shit," was all he could say. She had gotten more info than he had today, and he had thought he had a pretty good day.

Reese sat down on her bed again. "You need me. Gardner talks to me."

"A week, then you're out," he said, not wanting her there that long, but she might be right.

"A week, and you'll see you need me."

He pointed to her stuff in a messy pile on one side of the room. "You need a new roommate."

"Finally, you're right about something tonight." She grinned.

"She didn't even try to stop me from coming in," he said in a little amusement about how easy it was to get in here.

"I'm working on it. Gardi is looking for a place and needs a roommate. I was thinking about becoming homeless just as she finds a place." Reese was beyond smirking about her tidbit of information.

"Don't even think about it. She's slumming Reese. What is she even doing there?"

"I don't know. She didn't say. I'm there to make some real money for college."

"Don't move in with her," he demanded. "Promise me."

"I will if she asks. Better for me to live with her than some stranger. Am I right?"

"*Reese,*" he warned, but he knew she wasn't listening.

"Should I call you Declan or Daddy at work?"

"Sir, you can only address me as sir. And if you don't answer your phone, you will be fired." He pointed to it on the dresser charging.

"You can't fire a volunteer."

"Sure as shit I can."

He stormed out of her dorm room and headed for home. He

couldn't believe how tired he was after spending the entire day standing on his feet watching dudes watch tits. If he hadn't gotten to see Aurora so often, his day would have been shit. But he had been rewarded with two outfits on her gorgeous body. He knew that he was going to spend the night dreaming of taking both those outfits off of her, slowly.

CHAPTER
Eleven

IN AURORA'S LIFE, Friday night was now laundry night. It used to be cruising the bars with Win night or, visiting her clubs night, or visiting the competition night. Now, it was laundry night full of loads of pink in all its shades.

Win spent Friday night with Daniel. Every Friday night was their night. Xander went to his mom's, and they could do anything at any time and anywhere. Aurora stayed home with her Millie.

Aurora was happy that Win had found someone and had gotten married, but what she wouldn't give to cruise the bars one more time. But they couldn't even run out and get drinks because they were both recovering alcoholics. Her date was now Millie. She didn't drink alcohol either, so it worked out.

Sitting on the floor looking out at the city lights below her, Aurora folded all of Millie's little pants and shirts. Aurora had done more laundry for her daughter than she had ever done for herself. In the past she had been the queen of dry cleaning. She did one load of laundry every three weeks, in total. Now she did a load a week, usually two.

Pulling a t-shirt from her daughter's mouth, Aurora laughed at her.

It might not be the night she wanted, but she loved it anyway. Snuggling Millie into a hug, she almost cursed when the phone rang. Almost…because she was working on that. It had taken one little angel to make her realize what a potty mouth she had.

Looking at the number, she answered, "Aurora."

"There's an issue here," the familiar voice said.

Aurora went through her mental list of who was working, but neither of the little tit brigade should be there. Those were the two she worried most about. The rest were able to handle themselves in most situations.

"What?" Aurora asked, sitting the baby up on her lap and making her clap her little hands.

Trish didn't hold back, "A guy grabbed Char, and she punched him. He says he's pressing charges, and the cops are coming."

Everyone knew the rules."How did he touch her?"

"Not really sure because it was in the back room. I already called Chuck to look at the tapes."

"I'll be there soon," she said before hanging up.

It was Friday, and she had no sitter. Looking into the baby's gray eyes, she felt the pressure of being a single parent with no dad to help her out. Not for the first time did she think she needed a nanny. She couldn't afford a nanny, and the apartment was way too small for nannies.

But no matter how much she wanted a nanny tonight, she didn't have one. So, she would have to bring Millie with her. It wasn't ideal, but right now it was the only option.

Strapping Millie into her car seat, Aurora was happy she had changed into leggings and an oversized sweater earlier because she didn't want to waste time changing clothes. The cops were coming, and she was already half an hour away.

As she left the apartment, she glanced at Win's door, wishing she could leave the baby there. But this was their special night, and she wouldn't interfere with that.

By Thursday evening, Win and Aurora were over the argument of Wednesday night. No matter what they fought about, it didn't last long. Neither had apologized for what was said or thought the other needed to say one. They always just moved on; the fight might come back again one day, but it might not. They both had tempers that went off, and both were too stubborn to talk about it later. It worked for them.

Millie was a happy car baby. She always road nicely. Might be due to the fact that Daniel's parents lived half an hour from the apartment, so she was used to car trips. Or maybe it was because she was Aurora's baby, and Aurora loved car trips.

As she turned the BMW off the freeway, she saw cop cars surrounding the club as though someone had robbed it. Cops always came in large numbers when called to a strip club. Dialing the phone, she requested one of the waitresses come out and stay with Millie in the car. Or, actually, drive her around. There were a lot of lights that would keep her happy.

Once Aurora was in the lot, she pulled as close to the door as possible and climbed out as Gardi came running to her. The girl looked like she always did at work. Luckily, she had taken Aurora's advice and bought cheap jeans, if paying over a hundred for them was cheap. But that was far closer than what she had worn to the interview.

"I'm supposed to meet you out here?" Gardi asked in confusion.

Aurora knew the girl was not on the schedule, but here she was. "Really? I can't deal with you right now. What I need is for you to drive my car around. Make sure the baby doesn't cry or anything. Once the cops start leaving, you can come back."

"What?" Gardi's eyes were wide as if she didn't understand a word Aurora had said.

"Car, baby, drive." She pushed the younger woman into the driver's seat.

At least she knew this one wouldn't take off with her BMW. She probably had four at home, newer and better.

Walking into the club, it was nearly deserted, and the cops were everywhere. *Everywhere.* All employees were sitting at tables near the bar. Char was with them. Marching past the cops, she wanted to talk to Char first, which was exactly what she did. Cops could wait.

"What happened, Char?" she asked when she got to the table.

"I was giving him a lap dance, and he grabbed my boob and wouldn't let go. I asked again and when nothing happened, so I decked him," Char said.

Aurora tapped her foot as she thought. Char would have been alone, with no witnesses. Well, there was one. "Is Chuck coming in?"

"I called, but I haven't heard back," Tiff stated unhappily.

"Perfect, just perfect." *Now what?*

"Miss Carlyle," a cop said from behind her.

Spinning around, she asked with a bright smile, "Officer, what can I help you with?"

"Your girl decked Mr. Porter for no reason," the cop said with a smirk.

"Char wouldn't do that. He touched her. That is against my rules."

"Were you here to enforce the rule?"

"No, I was not."

"So, rules get broken?"

"I trust my girl way more than I trust your man over there. Char has been here for four years and has never been in any trouble." Aurora defended her girls to the end, as long as they deserved defending.

"Do you have any proof of that? We don't have all night." The cop was getting on her last nerve.

"My video guy is currently not responding to his calls." Aurora hated to tell this man that.

"I can take a look and see if I can figure out the system," Declan's voice came from by the door.

"I don't think you can figure it out, Declan." She shook her head. This was not some simple VCR system.

She'd invested big money into the system two years before, so much so that she couldn't begin to figure it out herself. Declan might think he was good with electronics, but she was sure this was also beyond him. She needed Chuck right now.

"Let me take a look. The cops aren't going to wait around for Chuck to show up," he insisted, and he was right. She had no choice.

"Fine, you can look. What little good that would do," she mumbled, walking down the hallway to what should have been her office but was now packed with digital surveillance equipment. Thousands of dollars of it.

"Impressive," was all he said as he walked into the room.

He took the seat that Chuck usually sat in and looked at everything for a while, taking it all in.

The officer came and leaned against the door jam and watched as Declan started to push buttons. After a few minutes, he had the correct camera images on the screen.

It had only taken him half an hour to show the cop that Mr. Porter was the one in the wrong. Char had been left no choice but to deck the man to get free. Porter had little to say when the evidence was in front of him and left quickly. As the cop gathered all his friends to leave, Aurora was left alone with Declan in the warm little room.

"I should have hired you for your computer knowledge. Have you used this system before?" she asked as he set everything right again.

"No, but it seemed easy enough." He grinned at her because he was lying to her.

"Why the fuck was the princess here?" she asked him as if he would know the answer. But now that the cops were gone, Gardi working this late at night was her biggest problem.

He acted dumb. "Princess?"

"Gardi, she was supposed to be off at four today. I can't have her working on Friday night."

"I think she was picking up a shift from another girl," Declan stated.

"Fuck, now I have to tell them not to let her work Friday or Saturday nights. Imagine if it had been her in that room with handsy Porter? Char punched him. The princess would still be in there."

"Why do you call her princess?" he asked.

"Really, cop? Her jeans cost more than she makes at this place in a week. And don't get me started on the jewelry." She leaned against the wall, trying to get the images of Gardi trapped with that guy out of her mind.

"I'm not a cop," he said very quietly.

He had gotten up, and they were very close in the small room, too close.

Her eyes caught his. "A cop that can look me in the eye and lie."

"When did I lie?" he stated, hating that he had to lie to her. But he had no idea why Gardner was working for her and until he did, he had to continue.

"You just lied. You have a tell." She watched his eyebrow go up in question, she tried not to focus on his lip that always betrayed him.

"What is it?" he asked, stepping even closer to her.

"I can't tell you."

He was too close. Aurora was having trouble thinking, breathing.

"Because I don't have a tell?" he whispered as his hand slipped up her arm and touched the ends of her hair.

"It's like a neon sign every time you lie." Watching his fingers play with the platinum strands, she knew she should jerk away but couldn't gather the energy to do it.

"I have to kiss you, Aurora."

And he did. Not as demanding as it was in the parking lot so long ago, but a small taste. And man, he tasted good, too good. Which was why she had been dreaming of this for a month now.

Pulling him tighter to her, to feel as much of him as she could as his tongue slipped past her lips, she groaned at the taste of him. It brought back flashes from the night in the parking lot, and she wanted a repeat of it. But more.

"Aurora, Gardi is back with your car. She wants to know what to do now," Tiff's voice was coming down the hallway toward the office, fast.

Aurora pushed him away from her like she was a teen caught with a boy in her bedroom. Fuck, that had never happened. But he was an employee, and what had just happened was a big no-no.

"Coming," she called and looked into his gray eyes.

He didn't look guilty at all. In fact, he looked the complete opposite of guilty.

Turning away with a growl of anger, she walked away from the office and him. Back in the bar, she looked around her empty club at nine p.m. on a Friday night. The place should be full, but there were only a handful of regulars still there. No cop was kicking them out of their titty bar.

Looking over her employees, she sent a quarter of them home. No need for so many people tonight. It would pick up in an hour or so, but it wouldn't be the usual Friday night crowd. Telling them that she would send Gardi home when she talked to her, Aurora crossed to the exit.

Without looking for Declan, because she didn't care about him, she walked out of her club. Gardi was still sitting in her SUV, right near the door where she had picked it up less than an hour ago.

Getting into the passenger seat, she asked, "How is Millie?"

"Sleeping, only in the past few minutes," Gardi said.

Aurora looked into the back seat, and sure enough, Millie's head was cocked to the side, and she was sound asleep. Her baby was not up for late nights with her mom yet.

"Thanks, Gardi. I couldn't bring her in there with the cops." Aurora gave an involuntary shake at the word cop. Even though she had just had one's tongue down her throat minutes before.

"I understand. What is her name?" Gardi looked back at her sleeping baby with an excitement only Gardi could pull off as normal.

Ignoring that Gardi would understand anything that had happened in the club tonight, she answered the question, "Millie, she's just over a year now."

"Do you ever bring her to the club?" Gardi wrapped her fingers around the steering wheel.

"I do. I used to more, when she was nursing. But in the last few months, I've been concentrating on being home more. So, those times when I used to bring her in now I try to trust my staff more and stay home." Aurora said.

"I can't see her in the club."

"She fits in pretty good. I mean, her Rising Passions t-shirt is more revealing than a mom wants to see, but it's the uniform," Aurora joked with her.

"What?" Eyes wide in confusion, Gardi didn't get it.

"I was kidding, Gardi. The girls love to see her, and I barely see her when I bring her in. They are just passing her around," Aurora said with a laugh. She loved gullible people. They were fun.

"I knew that," the girl lied but didn't look away from her.

"Sure, you did. What were you doing here tonight?" Aurora looked at the kid who, after a month, hadn't gotten used to being a waitress yet but still hadn't quit.

"Kylie called in sick. Tiff asked if anyone wanted to stay. I had nothing going on, so I stayed," Gardi explained.

"You shouldn't have put in a double. And I don't want you working Friday or Saturday night." She didn't add that it got too busy for everyone to keep an eye on her on top of their usual jobs.

"I can do it, Aurora," Gardi defended herself.

"Gardi, what would you have done if that guy had grabbed your boob? He wasn't letting go when Char punched him. Would you be able to defend yourself?" Aurora asked.

"Yes, I could," Gardi said with so much conviction that Aurora was sure the kid believed it.

"Go home, Gardi. The place is dead now, so you aren't needed." Aurora opened the door, and Gardi got out of her SUV.

Grabbing the open door, the girl said, "Good night, Aurora." And headed back to the building.

At her door, Aurora watched her push her way into the club and disappear. That girl still didn't know how dangerous this place could be. Sure, Aurora worked hard to keep it safe and secure for everyone, but there was only so much she could control.

Moving around from the passenger to the driver seat, Aurora glanced at Millie to see if she was still innocently sleeping in the back seat. She was. Pulling out of the lot, she saw Gardi leaving the club with Declan following her. At least they were listening to her about escorting her to her car. That was at least something.

The drive back to her apartment gave Aurora time to think about the kiss. She'd known it was coming, and still, she let it happen. Still wanted it to happen. Because his touch was what she had been craving for a so long now, and having him near had intensified her feelings.

Why did he have to be the man who was replacing the memory of that other man in her mind? It was now him she thought of before she fell asleep. Since that night, she hadn't looked at Indulge to see if he'd rejoined the service.

The only good that could come out of this was that she would stop thinking about "what might have been" with the mystery man. But she would always have a reminder of him. She had Millie.

CHAPTER
Twelve

IT WAS SATURDAY, and Declan didn't have to work until four in the afternoon, but Gardi worked at ten in the morning. Today, he had to leave watching her up to others all day. Reese was working the same shift, Nick was in the bar, and Rex was in the parking lot. It was covered, but Declan hated giving up so much control.

Reese was turning out to be a better asset than he had ever thought she would be. They could lay off having a guy in the bar all the time with her there. And almost every day she worked with Gardner, she came away knowing what the girl was doing for the next day or two. They were even texting each other now. Like real friends.

Today at one, he'd had a meeting with Royal Westmoreland about his daughter. Declan hadn't known if he should tell Royal what his daughter was up too. He had expected the man to be mad and put a stop to it. But instead, Royal had chuckled about the fact that she was working at a strip club, as long as she was not stripping. Then he quickly moved onto wondered why she was at the law office. No wonder about the club at all. That seemed obvious to her father. But he wasn't sharing that with the man he'd hired to keep her safe.

After being told to keep it up, he was dismissed. No end date set, nothing. He didn't know if he would have to guard this kid until he died, but at least the money was good.

Since he had nothing to do between the meeting and work, he went to the club early. It was getting busy, and Reese and Gardi were both keeping very busy. Aurora wasn't there, but he heard she rarely came in on the weekends anymore, only for emergencies.

And she had a kid. When Gardner said she was driving the car because her kid was in it, Declan was shocked. Maybe it was a step-kid or an adopted kid? Gardi had given him very little information on the kid on the walk to her car the night before, mostly because she didn't know Declan from any of the other bouncers, even if Declan knew everything about Gardner.

When he thought about the kid, all Declan could picture was a platinum-blonde little kid with a tight skirt and heels. That was exactly what Aurora's kid would look like. She would be fucking adorable and full of sass like her mom.

But how old was the kid? He wondered as he stood by the door. It had to be older but not old enough to be alone. Two years before, she said she was a lonely stay-at-home mom. The mom part must have been true. Because she was not staying at home, she already had a strip club empire at the time. But that didn't mean she didn't have the kids.

Wishing she would come in, he watched the crowd to make sure none were doing anything they shouldn't. He glanced at her booth, but it was empty. After working there for more than a few days, he realized it was empty more than it was full. And when she was here, she was working. Papers and her computer were usually scattered around her, and her concentration was on those. Even though she took in everything around her, without anyone ever noticing it.

After getting the job and being able to watch Gardner on the inside, he realized there had been no reason for more than one person to be in the club, much less two guys. With every other employee making sure Gardner wasn't being harassed by anyone, a single person could do what two had done before. Which was a good thing since he was down four men now. It seemed a strip club was the ultimate testing ground for PIs. He would have to hire more employees before this was over.

And with Reese having nearly the exact same schedule as Gardner, he didn't even feel needed. He was spending more time watching men and some women come and go from the club than watching Gardner when he worked. Or working the wrong shift entirely.

Aurora had packed his schedule. He was going to be here a lot. He deserved it after his performance when she hired him since she did the scheduling. But all he wanted to do was see Aurora when he was in here, and the days she wasn't there were a disappointment.

That minx was doing it on purpose. Of course, she knew exactly what she was doing. This was punishment for his being a cop. No matter how many times he said he wasn't, she wasn't buying it.

His eyes looked over the crowd, but his mind was on her body pressed against his last night. As hot and sexy as it always was when he touched her. What he wouldn't give to have just shut that door and slid off her clothes, seeing that gorgeous body again. See if it had changed since the last time he had seen the entire thing in a hotel room downtown two years before. Sure, they'd had sex in the parking lot that night, but he hadn't even got to see her breasts. And he liked those.

Back then, it was only about sex because they had barely talked. And still, he hadn't been able to forget her. Now he knew her personality, and he knew he wasn't walking away from her this time. Once this Gardner thing was over, he was going to take her out and do it right. She deserved it.

CHAPTER
Thirteen

SUNDAY, just before lunch, Aurora crossed the hallway with Millie. The door was already open so she let herself in, only to drop her daughter off in the middle of Win's apartment, before going back for her briefcase and computer. It was accounting day.

Every month on Sunday afternoon, Aurora got together with Win to go over her books. They had been doing it since Aurora bought her first club and had been extremely nervous about getting it wrong for the feds. Now she was confident enough that she didn't need to have her numbers-expert friend look over them every month. But now, it was a ritual more than actual work. It had been years since Win had found anything so wrong that it would cost her in the end.

By the time she had gotten all her stuff to Win's, Win still hadn't shown up in the main part of the apartment yet. Chalking it up to married life, Aurora grabbed the toys in a basket for Millie to play with. Sitting down with the baby, she was glad she had worn the gray leggings and red sweater so she was comfortable as Millie pulled out toy after toy from the basket. Every few toys, she would bring one over to her mom and show her, very close to Aurora's eyes.

Win finally came out from the back bedroom, and she was smirking as she shut the bedroom door behind her. She was wearing almost the exact same outfit as Aurora, just a different color top, which made them laugh at each other.

"Sorry about that. I had to finish something," Win said, grabbing Aurora's briefcase from the table.

"You're a devil. Is he already sleeping?" Aurora got up off the floor.

"Not quite." Win pulled out Aurora's computer. They had been doing this for a long time.

"At least he won't be in the way while you do my books." Aurora laughed as she grabbed a water and bottle of pop from her friend's fridge, like always.

"He should be out of the way for a while. And later, he has to go get Xander." Win opened the laptop and typed the password in.

Setting the bottles down, Aurora looked over at the baby, who was just playing with some blocks. Sitting down, she asked, "How is this Xander thing going?"

"What do you mean?" Win asked, not looking up as she found the programs she wanted to use.

"Having a kid around all the time? The whole mom thing?" Aurora opened her water.

Win looked up at her words. "He's good. It's been almost two years now. I always thought the co-parenting thing was going to be hard, but I like to send him off for a few days. Get my Mac time."

Aurora was glad she hadn't taken a drink of water when Win said that: Mac time means bedroom time. When they met through the same app Aurora had found Millie's dad on, Daniel's screen name was Mac, and Win's was Fred, and when they didn't think anyone was around, they called each other by those names. It was cute and uncomfortable all at the same time.

"A few days off. What I wouldn't give." Aurora glanced over at the baby.

"We can take her every once in a while, Aurora. So, you can date." Win always offered, but Aurora hadn't taken her up on it much. The baby was her responsibility—and hers alone.

"Why would I waste time alone for dating, Win? Fucking and sleeping, that is how I would fill that time," Aurora said and slammed her hand over her mouth.

No swearing around the kid.

Win just laughed at her. "Do we need a swear jar, Rora?"

"I would go broke," Aurora admitted.

"Do you have someone in mind for the not sleeping part of your free time?" Win asked.

"No," Aurora said too quickly.

"You can't lie to me, Aurora. Twenty years says you can't lie to me," Win said, pushing the computer away from her. "The bouncer?"

"I don't do that with my employees," Aurora stated, wishing she could swear.

"Like you have any rules on it. Your employees do it all the time," Win pointed out.

"You make it sound like they don't at least try and hide it from me. Because they do." Aurora didn't like to see it but knew it had happened. Hell, she had former employees who were married to each other.

"I'm just saying. Do it." Win laughed and held up her pop bottle to toast her, but Aurora didn't respond in kind.

"There is something going on, and he's a part of it. He's a..." She stopped and looked at Millie on the floor. "A cop."

Win chuckled at her words. "Most likely not anymore. And maybe you can forgive him a little for the cop thing since you're basically a car thief. In recovery, but a car thief."

"Really, of all my sins of youth, car thief is what sticks in your mind, Winter?"

"I do believe that car thief is the only one you still do," Winter said with a smirk.

"I do not," she argued.

"My Buick has almost a thousand more miles than when I last drove it," Win pointed out.

"You should drive it more. How do you even know it has more miles on it?"

Win tapped her head. "Numbers, Rora."

Aurora leaned back in her chair and folded her arms. She was caught. Completely caught. "Your car smells, Winter."

"It only smells because your car still smells new. It's been years and still smells new," Win said.

"I take care of my car. Unlike you."

"I don't even want that car. I just can't find the keys to get rid of it. Do you have the keys?" Win asked.

"Fuck no, keys are optional." Aurora laughed and then slammed her hand to her mouth.

"Will you teach me one day?" Win asked

"No, Winter, I won't. You stay out of the seedy underbelly of this city."

"I used to live there." Win pointed out. She had spent a year homeless before ending up in reform school.

"Not long enough, sweetheart," Aurora said, wishing Win hadn't spent any time there. She didn't need to know what it was like at all.

"Do you think we ever ran into each other when we were out there and not realized it?" Win asked.

"No, you were cocaine, I was meth, our roads didn't cross."

"But you never used it. I mean, just wondering around."

"You were only homeless for a year. I was already in ten months before you even showed up. That left only two months. I don't think we did. But we would be unstoppable drug lords now if we had." Aurora laughed at the image. In reality, they would either be dead or in prison, probably dead. And most likely a long time ago.

"We could have ruled this city," Win said, looking out the big windows at the city in question.

"Are you still going to see your dad?" Aurora followed her gaze. They may not own it, but they had made it far above it.

"Yes, we leave on Friday." Win pulled the computer toward her.

"Penny and Henry are going somewhere also. She told me on Friday. So, I have to find someone for my Millie." Aurora looked over to her daughter, who paid no attention to the adults in the room.

"Yeah, once they heard we were going away, they wanted to go to Europe somewhere for the week. I won't know where until we get a souvenir spoon or something from them when they come back." Win analyzed the numbers as she spoke.

"I better get a fucking spoon from both of you guys," Aurora said.

This was one of the first vacations Win had taken without her, except for her honeymoon.

"I'm going like two hours from here. What spoon?"

"I expect one from their fancy silverware drawer. And it better have a fucking R on it." Win's family name was Ramstad.

"I'll grab you one the first meal they serve me," Win easily agreed.

"You had better."

"You started swearing again."

"I have no way to control it," Aurora admitted. "She's going to be kicked out of preschool for swearing. And just think of high school. I was suspended for swearing. Four times."

"You have time before she's kicked out of school," Win said

"I think she already said fuck, it was completely wrong, but the context was right. I'm not winning at parenthood." In defeat, Aurora slouched into her chair.

"You're killing it as a parent, because you're either working or with your kid. You sold one of your clubs for her."

"Friday night, I had to bring her to the club. The cops were called," Aurora admitted. Win knew that Aurora was automatically called when the cops came.

"You brought her inside during an arrest?"

"No, I had a waitress drive her around while I took care of everything. But I brought her."

"And it went fine; you have staff you can boss around. You could have dropped her off. We were home."

"It was Friday. That's your day," Aurora pointed out. "I take advantage of you guys so much as it is."

"We love having her. Xander loves her. And we both understand your job isn't the same as ours. I can walk out of work at five and not think about it until morning. But you're on call at all times. I've never been disappointed to wake up to her in my kitchen." Win pointed at the crib that was always up.

"Lately, it's felt like a lot. I'm gone a lot. What happens when you move to the burbs?" she pointed out.

"We are not moving. You'll be moving first."

"I'll never see you if you have to schedule time for me. And you will never drive to the club for classes when you move. You don't drive."

"I'm not moving."

"Would you take a self-defense class if I offered them at the club?" Aurora asked. She had been thinking about it since the fight on Friday night. Maybe some of her girls needed to know how to defend themselves.

"No, but I'm sure you will make me go. I might even like it. Just don't make it two hours long," Win said without looking up.

"It's definitely going to be two hours," Aurora said.

"Who is going to teach it?"

"I don't know yet. It's just in the beginning stages."

"Are you inviting the public?"

"No, they won't come."

"I think they would. Self-defense, and they can see inside a strip club. You know housewives want a peek," Win said, still looking at something, then typing something.

"They want to but won't do it."

Aurora wanted to know what she was typing but didn't ask. Win never liked to be micromanaged. Odd, because that was what her job was: micromanaging.

"Are you ladies having a marketing meeting?" Daniel asked, walking into the kitchen all smiles.

"Yes," Win said, not looking up at her husband, but he definitely looked at her.

"We are debating whether men like tits or asses better." Aurora loved razing Daniel.

"I, as a man, prefer tits. But only these." He grabbed his wife's and shook them.

"You're no longer my demographic." Aurora laughed at Win's anger at her husband's actions. She had been too engrossed in her numbers to have been paying attention to what he was doing or saying until he touched her.

"She wants to offer a self-defense class." Win pushed away his hands when they lingered on her breast too long.

"Your girls are pretty tough already, Aurora. But maybe some could use it." Daniel kissed his wife's head.

"Win thinks the public would be interested. I say no." Aurora turned her attention to him. Win was looking at the numbers again.

"Maybe start with a one-time thing, a weekend afternoon, and see if you get any takers. You can always turn it to only employees if no one shows." Daniel sounded serious. He was, after all, the director of marketing at the tech company where he and Win worked.

"Is this how you act at work, all smart?" Aurora questioned him, trying to get him to laugh.

"Yes, because I am smart. Win wouldn't want me if I wasn't." This time, there was no hint of laughter.

She didn't smirk but wanted to. "I know why Winter wants you."

"Me too." His face didn't break.

"Big cock." She maintained her straight face.

He didn't break. "That's right."

"Jesus Christ, you two. Stop. No talk of cock in the kitchen. During a meeting with Millie here." Win interrupted them, making them both break down laughing.

"I have to get Xander," Daniel said when he recovered, kissed his wife, and walked out of the apartment.

"Can we talk about cock now?" Aurora asked Win.

"If you want to. Just having you two talking about it is weird," Win said.

"You know I'm not interested in Daniel, right?" Aurora asked, never thinking Win would be jealous, but maybe.

In all their years together, they had never wanted the same man. Their tastes had always run in different directions for that.

"Of course not; you have a type." Winter looked through some papers she pulled from Aurora's briefcase.

"I do not." Aurora pushed up her arms in denial.

"Okay, Rora," Win said, looking over at Millie playing on the floor.

Aurora followed her gaze. "That was a one-time thing."

"Just saying the bouncer and the baby seem to have something in common. Tall, dark, and handsome," Win said.

Looking over at the baby, Aurora was willing to admit maybe she had a type. "I'll have you know I've done things with a rainbow of men."

"I do love it when you're trying not to swear. And not in years, like ten. Always dark-haired, always." Win put down the papers and looked at Aurora.

"Not always." She tried again with her argument.

"I knew what the baby was going to look like long before she was born. I could have told you years ago what your baby was going to look like." Winter looked at the baby again.

"Is it weird that she looks like you?" Aurora looked at her friend with her black hair and brown eyes.

Laughing, Win said, "If I had been a guy, we would have been married forever."

"I never thought about the fact that Daniel is blond, but he isn't as attractive as I am."

Win frowned. "I'm not secretly in love with you, Rora."

"I, sadly, am madly in love with you, but you're taken." Aurora laughed as Win stuck her tongue out at her.

"That I am, and I like cock." Win shrugged. "So your records are perfect, again. Are we doing this again next month, or are you going to just skip these little meetings?"

"We're never stopping because this is the only time I get to eat Chinese," Aurora pointed out. They always ordered Chinese, something she never ordered any other time.

"I'll send you a bill." Win was putting the computer back in the briefcase.

"I'll promptly ignore it, so get your past due one ready right away." Aurora laughed; it was actually an automatic payment to Win's account.

"I'll send them in the same envelope." Win got up and went to get new beverages for them.

"Are you knocked up yet?" Aurora asked when Win's face was in the fridge.

Win slammed the fridge shut. "I'm not."

"You can't tell your daddy first. I deserve to be told first, even before that guy you married." Aurora took the water bottle from her.

"I'm not pregnant, you will be told second, after that guy I married." Win sat back down.

"I told you first," Aurora pointed out.

"You still haven't told the guy to this day." Win looked at Millie, still entertaining herself.

Aurora shrugged. She would have if she had been able to find him. Maybe. "Are you nervous about the trip? You haven't been back since you were fourteen or fifteen."

"I was fourteen, and yes, I am. At least Daniel is coming, so I won't be alone." Win put down her bottle on the table.

"I would go if you want me to," Aurora said, knowing she shouldn't leave her clubs but would if Win asked. She would do anything for Win, no questions asked.

"No, you stay here. Then I'll have someone to tell all my stories to," Win said.

"You just think your parents wouldn't approve of our friendship," Aurora said.

"They already met you. And they like you," Win said, but they both knew it wasn't the truth.

"They thought I was a hooker," Aurora pointed out.

"You told them you were a hooker."

"They deserved it. I think the youngest boy had a boner the entire day." Aurora laughed at the memory of the teen's eyes on her the entire day.

"I don't want to know. He's my brother," Win said, trying to sound angry and failing.

"What was his name?"

"Ridge."

"Your parents are such hippies. They don't look it, but really." Aurora listed them on her fingers. "Winter, Summer, Autumn, Ridge, and the other one."

"Forrest."

"I hope the boys didn't get Rose as a middle name too." Aurora chuckled. All the girls had the same middle name.

"I don't know. If I ever knew, I've forgotten." Win took a drink of her pop.

"I'm just going to say that it is. Next time I see them, I'm going to call them all by their first and middle names."

"Go ahead." Win just shook her head before setting her bottle down on the table. "Have you ever looked for your mom?"

Agitated by the question, she got up to get the baby. "Hell no. What would I want to find that woman for?"

"Closure," Win pointed out. It was probably something she learned in therapy.

Picking up Millie, she said, "I've closed that chapter of my life so hard that the book fell right into the trash. I have this new book, and I love it."

"Maybe she had reasons for what she did," Win said as Aurora danced her baby back to the table.

"She had her reasons: money, alcohol, drugs, and sex. Not always in that order, but all were usually there." Aurora dipped the baby at Win.

"Just saying." Win tickled the baby, who was tipped at her, making her giggle.

"Don't. I never had that happy childhood you had, Winter. Mine sucked. If I did find her, she wouldn't be inviting me upstate for the week to enjoy pleasant days reminiscing about the good times. I would probably be visiting her in jail, and she would be asking me to bring in smokes and a file in a cake." Aurora danced back to her chair.

Win laughed at the image Aurora painted. "Would your grandma be there?"

"Ohh yeah, a family fucking reunion." Aurora put her hands over the baby's ears as she said it.

The fun was interrupted by a knock on the door announcing that the Chinese food was there. Win paid the man and brought the food to the table as Aurora grabbed plates and silverware. Gone were the days of eating it straight from the box. Because they were adults now. Or maybe it was because Daniel complained when they did.

The conversation about families and the past was over as they ate and Aurora fed the baby. It was a comforting meal they both looked forward to during the week. Sometimes Daniel was there, sometimes not. Millie was now always there.

When Daniel arrived home with Xander, the boy took over the conversation as only a six-year-old could. He was all chatter about his weekend and what his life was like with his mom. Any tension about family visits was erased.

Once the meal was over, Aurora took Millie home and left Win alone with her little family. No matter what happened in life, Aurora hoped that they would still get together on Sunday afternoons, even if they didn't have accounting work to do.

CHAPTER
Fourteen

DECLAN HAD no idea what he was going to say to Aurora if she actually opened the door. An hour ago, he had gone out for a drive. He had driven past Gardner's father's mansion. The kid was safely tucked away for the night. Rex was in his car on the street, just in case. With her safe, he just let himself drive without a destination in mind. Until he was pulling into a parking spot twenty-five floors below where Aurora lived.

Looking up at the building, he knew he had no reason to be there. Not a one. No reason to walk into the building, no reason to punch the twenty-five in the elevator. No reason to be knocking on her door.

But he was doing it anyway. The last time he had seen her, he had kissed her, and he was still thinking about it, and it had been days. He was going to see her again tomorrow. On Mondays, she was at the club all afternoon, and he was on schedule. But he didn't want to just see her. He wanted more.

Walking down the carpeted hallway, he was fifty percent sure that she was going to fire him tonight just for showing up at her door. Would she question how he got her address? It could jeopardize his case with Gardner.

But his dick was in charge tonight. His dick was winning. And boy, was he happy when she swung the door open and shot him a sassy smile instead of anger.

She leaned against the door jam. "Fancy meeting you in my hall-way, cop."

"Just in the neighborhood." His eyes swept her from her bare feet with their red painted toenails to her blond hair in a ponytail. *She had it in a ponytail.* Her gray leggings and red sweater hugged her curves and gave him a taste of what was below. A taste that wasn't enough.

Her eyes trailed down his body, taking him in. "I bet. Shouldn't you be working?"

"Not today, boss lady. You finally gave me a day off." Taking a small step closer to her, he reached out and rested his hand on the door jam just above her head.

"You didn't deserve it." She stood her ground, even if her toes curled into the carpet below her feet.

"What do I deserve?" Taking another step toward her so they were almost touching, he finally smelled the sweet scent of her perfume.

"To fuck me." Grabbing his jacket, she pulled him so their lips crashed into each other.

Pushing her into the apartment, he slammed the door behind him, never lifting his mouth from hers. He couldn't stop kissing her if the apartment was on fire, mostly because he wouldn't notice. Sliding his hands up her body and under her red sweater to cup the breasts that he had been dreaming about for so long, he groaned into her mouth.

Cursing, he pulled his lips from hers just long enough to pull the shirt over her head. Looking down at her red bra, he groaned. He had missed them. Reaching behind her, he unclasped the bra, easily this time, and was rewarded by seeing the full pale globes with their pert pink nipples. For the last few days, he had seen nothing but tits, but they were nothing compared to these. These were the only ones that turned him on in an instant.

While he was admiring her rack, she pushed off the jacket and flannel shirt he had been wearing. Before they hit the ground, she was pushing the grey t-shirt over his head. Her eyes looked at his chest and stomach as her hands touched them. "I didn't know they let cops work out."

A warm hand slid into his jeans and slid across his skin until she grasped the button in her fist. Her fingertips grazed his steel-hard cock. Hand still holding his pants, she pulled him across her dimly lit apartment. It was a spacious apartment, but Declan wasn't paying attention to any of it, just her naked breasts as she walked backward toward her bedroom.

Once there, her hands made quick work of shedding his jeans and boxers almost as fast as he had gotten rid of hers. Since he hadn't been able to look at her in the parking lot, he took the time to explore her curves and touch every inch of her at his leisure.

She had changed slightly over the last year, but not her smell, her taste, her touch. Everything was the same. It was like coming home to be back in her arms. Back where he belonged.

Pushing her gently onto the bed, he climbed in after her, running a hand up her entire body, touching every inch of her he could. He whispered, "You're perfect."

"And you're a cop, a cop without a clue. Which doesn't matter right now because I need to be fucked, cop," she argued with him, her hand caressing his hard cock as she said the words.

"You need to be loved, Aurora, slow and lovingly." Finally, he took her nipple into his mouth, and her hand stilled.

"Flowery words for a cop," she moaned the words as his fingers slid down her body. Finding her wet, he easily slid across her clit.

With the memory of what she liked, he used just enough pressure to make her writhe and buck, and her mouth beg for more. Something he gave willingly, bringing her to her peak. Allowing him to watch the orgasm roll through her body. Her eyes closed as she moaned and writhed in his arms.

As her body started quivering from her orgasm, he sheathed himself with a condom before sliding into her core, causing her to moan and writhe again instantly.

Effortlessly finding rhythm, he moved with her on the soft, king-sized bed. He loved how responsive she was. How easily their bodies moved together. That their bodies seemed perfectly aligned.

Trying to hold off his orgasm as long as possible, especially after the parking lot, he enjoyed watching the orgasms roll through her nearly without stopping. He had never been with a woman who had multiple orgasms that rolled into one another. But his Aurora had them every time they were together.

Her inner walls were squeezing his cock until he couldn't control his reaction anymore. As his orgasm hit hard and fast, it was she who had gained control and was rocking against him, causing another orgasm to roll through her.

Shifting them onto their sides, neither could catch their breaths for a while. With her chest heaving, he wanted to tell her everything: about the case, about their past, everything. Instead, he said nothing and watched her sparkling green eyes as she rose over him, only to straddle him with a wicked grin.

Two minutes before, he had been sure he was done for the night, but Aurora's body, on full glorious display, had his dick ready for round two. Happily, Aurora was taking charge this time.

Fifteen

AFTER AURORA HAD KICKED Declan out just before sunrise, she had fallen back to sleep. Or to sleep, as the case may be. But it was worth it. A night of sex had been worth it.

Millie's cries woke her later than she had wanted to get up. Not that she had to be anywhere until noon, but she liked to be up before little Millie was. Rolling out of bed, she pulled a robe over her naked body and went to get her crying baby.

In the pink bedroom, Millie was standing in her crib, holding onto the railing with giant tears rolling down her face. She rescued her daughter from the hated crib. Carlyle's never liked being behind bars, and Millie was no different.

After changing the baby's diaper, Aurora took her to her bedroom so she could get ready for the day. Plopping the little thing on the bed, she picked her up again and looked down at her. She hadn't had a man in her bed since Millie was born. It was weird to put her there now. Instead, she put her on the floor and opened the basket of toys she kept in there.

Closing the door so Millie couldn't go into the rest of the apartment, Aurora changed the sheets and made the bed. Not that she still didn't see him there, and he was doing all those amazing things to her. Maybe she needed to change the sheets again after those thoughts?

Showered and ready for the day, Aurora fed Millie and cleaned up the apartment while the kid hand-fed herself a post-breakfast snack, still in her pink pajamas because she had no control over what she ate and what a mess it created.

Aurora cleaned up the toys in the bedroom and then went to the living room, which was mostly clean, but her laptop was there and a notebook. Win had gotten to her yesterday, and Aurora had started to look for her mom. Damn, Winter!

When Declan knocked, she thought she had found the correct Sylvia Carlyle, which was her grandmother, not her mom. But she had no luck with Debbie Carlyle yet. Taking the laptop to the table, she flipped it open, poured a few more baby crunches onto Millie's tray, and looked back at the page she had found.

Sadly, it was one of those family history pages that listed Sylvia as deceased. Aurora paid the price to see if a hundred dollars would buy her a glimpse into where she came from. Sylvia Carlyle had three kids; the first was Debra, and the others were Donnie and Dawn. Their names weren't ones that Aurora could dredge from her memory. All three had nothing but a birth date, meaning they were either alive or the site didn't know if they were dead.

Sylvia, on the other hand, was long dead. Dead before Aurora met Winter at fifteen. Dead in New Jersey within months of Aurora's arrest for the meth lab. Somehow, Aurora felt she should have already known of her death, just felt it.

Above her name on the site were what must have been her parents, but just her mother was listed. No father was listed. Seemed like single motherhood was a family tradition that went back generations. Aurora hoped that Millie would end that. Her baby was special. Aurora had always known that.

Writing down the date in her notebook, she would work on that angle later. Then she clicked on Debra's name to see if anything came up. Nothing great, but her birthdate was listed and the place of birth. Aurora wouldn't have guessed that she and her mom shared a birth month. Birthdays were not observed in her family.

What really surprised her was that her mom was only fifteen years older than she was. In her mind, her mom was way older, but her life had been a rough one. Checking back to Sylvia's information, she saw another pattern: teenage motherhood. What she didn't see was Debra having any more children, just one listed: Heaven, with Aurora's birthdate listed. There she was.

Slamming the computer closed in case Millie was watching what Aurora was doing, she took a deep breath. No way was Millie ever knowing who her grandmother had been. Maybe it was time to talk to Win about closing off that part of their lives from the children's hearing. It was time to make up some great childhood to spoon-feed her daughter until she was old enough to understand that what happened at fourteen doesn't have to affect who you are today.

Pulling Millie from the high chair, she went to change her daughter for the sitter. It was almost twelve, and she had to drive half an hour to Penny's place and then another fifteen minutes to the club. She was going to be late today. Good thing she didn't have to punch a clock.

In a pink sundress with a white sweater and adorable sandals, Millie was dropped off at the sitter. Penny oohed and ahhed over the outfit. Aurora loved it when she did that. Leaving her baby in the loving arms of the only grandmother she would ever know, Aurora headed to a seedier part of town and walked proudly into her club. She loved it here.

Trying to ignore Declan when she walked in, she glanced at his gorgeous body but tried not to stare. He had no such compunction and stared right at her ass all the way to her booth.

Today, she made next week's schedules for both clubs. Usually, she followed the same pattern as the week prior. People liked to have a set schedule. But next week, Win, Daniel, and Penny were going to be out of town. Aurora either had to take time off or find someone to watch Millie all week. But she didn't trust half of these people with her daughter.

Tapping through the program and adding and changing names and dates for her week off, she saw that a whiskey vendor was coming midweek. She always set those up on Wednesdays and always had them here. If one club did something, they all did. So, she would have to bring in Millie on Wednesday. That would be fine. But then she noticed that the tax man was coming on Tuesday to the other club. Millie and the tax man didn't sound like they would mix.

She put off scheduling for now since she had to think about how to get around having meetings and taking care of Millie at the same time. Aurora looked over the numbers from the weekend. To her shock, the incident on Friday night had cost her way more than she had expected. The attendance didn't pick up after the cops left. Guys could smell that the cops had been there. Aurora knew it. Hopefully, the other club didn't have a downturn in receipts.

After a few hours of disappointing numbers for the week, Tiff dropped the mail at Aurora's table. Aurora glanced through the pile and made two piles in front of her, one for bills and one for others. Most mail was bills. The others were usually things sent to every address in the city or random stuff. Sometimes, a letter would come from former employees or even customers. Today, there was only one letter like that.

The letter was addressed only to Carlyle, which was odd. She was usually just known as Aurora by all. Slipping the letter open, she read it and stopped breathing completely.

Heaven, if you don't give me $100,000, I'll tell your man exactly who and what you are, or else. A friend from your past.

Slamming the letter down, she looked around as if the letter hadn't come in the mail but had been said out loud. Who could have possibly found her now? She hadn't seen or heard from anyone from her past, ever. What secrets could they possibly tell about her? *Your man?* Looking up at Declan, she really couldn't consider him *her man*. They barely knew each other.

The whole thing seemed surreal. She had only had a man in her bed for twelve hours and had seen only a glimpse of her former name. But here they were in one letter sent days before.

There were instructions on the bottom of the paper instructing her to drop off the money in a suitcase in the park on Friday afternoon.

Last Friday. Looking at the postmark, it had been sent on Wednesday. What idiot thought it would get to her by Friday?

Deciding that it was a crackpot ex-employee or someone who came to the club. And since Friday was over, there was no need for her to worry. There had been no threat to her life or anything.

Before putting the letter in her briefcase in case she got another one, she glanced at it one more time. The only thing about it that caught her up was the Heaven part. Nobody knew that. Not even Win knew that. Maybe it was a mistake or a weird endearment.

Whatever it was, the time had passed, and nothing had happened. So, it didn't matter at all. Glancing at her phone, she saw that it was after five already, time to head home. Daniel would have picked up Millie with Xander already.

As she packed up her briefcase, she looked around at her employees. They were busy doing what they were supposed to do. This was her club, and she rarely had issues with the employees. Most had been here longer than at most strip clubs. The other club was completely different, with employee turnover being high.

Today, she was happy that the two young waitresses were not working. So far, she hadn't come up with why either woman was there. She had her suspicions but hadn't been able to confirm any of them. Maybe she should just fire them both before next week, but that would leave her short staffed. So, they would get another two weeks before she let them go. Both should probably be in college and working at the mall. Dating college boys and gossiping, not working here.

Declan was another story. She hadn't confirmed anything about his real identity either. She should really be more particular about who she brought home with Millie there. But her sense was that he wasn't dangerous or a criminal, just a cop. But why was he here at her club? When was he going to be moving on to his normal job?"

Sliding out of the booth, she waved goodbye to the bartender and a waitress who was waiting for drinks at the bar. Slinging the bag over her shoulder, she headed out of the club. The moment she was on her feet, her eyes caught Declan's and held them as she walked right toward him. How she managed the long walk without tripping on her feet, she didn't know because she was not watching where she was going at all, just him.

Once she made it to him, she walked right by without acknowledging him. Just like when she came in. No way was he getting special treatment because he had warmed her bed last night. No way was she letting that affect his work or hers.

Through the door, she walked into the sun, still keeping the city lit. Walking across the parking lot, she felt the familiar feeling of being watched. It had been over a month now. She had gotten used to it but still had no idea why it was happening. The hair on the back of her neck raised today, and her speed picked up. Should she have asked for an escort? From her own club? No way. This was her safe place.

Before she made it all the way to her SUV, Declan grabbed her arm and spun her around. "Why are you practically running?"

Trying to calm her racing heart, she looked up into his gray eyes. He must have been following her the entire time, making her think someone was following her.

Either way, she lied, "Just need to get home. I'm late."

"Late for what?" His hand remained around her arm but loose and became more intimate than before.

"I like to get home before six to spend time with my daughter," she admitted. She didn't lie about being a mother; she just didn't tell everyone about it the moment she met them.

"I didn't know you had a daughter," he said. Or actually, *he lied.*

Smirking, she said, "That I do."

He paused by her SUV. "Where was she last night?"

"Sleeping, she goes to bed before ten at night." She reminded him of the time he showed up at her door as she unlocked the door to her SUV.

"Will she be asleep tonight at ten?" he asked, his hand still around her arm, but the other one slipped around her waist.

"It's very possible," she whispered as his lips descended toward her.

So engrossed was she by him and his lips that it took her a moment longer than it should have to hit the ground at the sound of a gun going off somewhere close. If her mind had been working at one hundred percent, she wouldn't have needed him to pull her down. She even let him drag her to the front of her SUV as another shot rang out in the sunshine.

Her eyes were darting around, looking for where the shots could possibly be coming from. She saw nothing and sensed nothing. "Where's your gun, cop?" she hissed. His body pressed hers into the front of her SUV.

"You said no guns, boss," he hissed. He was pissed about it.

"I didn't think you'd listen to me," she said as a few men, including another of her bouncers, ran out of the building.

Within a minute, a cop car swerved into the parking lot. Blue lights blazing. This was going to fuck with her numbers again. Pushing Declan away from her, she had to get this cop gone before he completely destroyed her entire day.

"Where are you going?" He asked, resisting her efforts to get away.

"Getting this fucking cop off my property."

His hold released, and she pushed him completely off her. She straightened her dirty outfit and marched toward the cop car in the empty open part of the lot.

The cop was out of the car with his gun out already. "We got a call of shots fired."

"Put that away, officer, whoever it was is gone," She stated. If they weren't, they would have shot again.

The cop didn't put away his gun as he looked around. "Who do you think it was?"

"I don't know, probably just some whack job. This isn't the best neighborhood. I'm sure it won't happen again," Aurora made her argument. Get his guy gone.

"You were shot at, ma'am?" The officer asked, looking her over a little too closely for her comfort.

"No, I wasn't. It was just wild shots, nothing even close to me." Aurora folded her arms over her chest as the men who had come out of the club hurried to their cars.

"Two shots were fired; the first one hit the SUV, and the other didn't. I don't think they were wild shots," Declan stated from beside her.

"Just a coincidence," Aurora argued as two patrons drove off with her profits.

"Did you see anything?" the officer asked Declan more than her. Aurora was being dismissed.

"No, I didn't. It just came out of nowhere," Declan said, looking around the lot again.

"It was nothing," Aurora stated louder than she needed to, but no one was listening to her. "So, you can leave."

"I should look around," the cop said, but he was really looking at Declan. *Fuck the cop thing.*

"No need. It's just the neighborhood. I'll have security stepped up," she said as her night manager pulled into the lot. Brendon would be able to take care of this.

Declan drew her aside. "I think you might be in shock. It happens. We'll figure this out."

He called to one of the waitresses to get her a drink of water and the first-aid kit. Aurora rolled her eyes. She'd been taking care of herself for longer than most of her staff had been alive. She didn't need anyone watching out for her. Even if he did have a great ass.

Once the third man was in the conversation, she was completely shut out of it. Despite her being the center of the entire interaction they didn't even bother to talk to her. Over the years, she had grown used to it, but it still ticked her off. This was her fucking business, not her manager's or her bouncer. In fact, she was the one that was shot at. But none of them had any time for her, even if she had the most stake in the entire situation.

Well, fine, she looked at them all one more time and turned to see this hole in her SUV. She discovered it was only in the back bumper. Picking up her briefcase from the ground, she put it in the back seat. Slamming the door, she saw that none of the men had even noticed she wasn't near them anymore. Shrugging, she got in the SUV herself and started the engine. When no one looked her way. She left.

Within a few minutes, she got a call from her bouncer, Brandon, but she told him to take care of it before every patron she had was gone. Pushing the thought that someone was trying to harm her from her mind, she drove through the city. Maybe she should trade in her SUV for a little less fancy vehicle. This could have been about her expensive SUV.

Or maybe they thought that she had money on her. But why didn't that person reveal themselves to get the money? No, it was just a random thing.

After parking the SUV in its parking spot, she looked at the little hole again. Her chest constricted. Next week, she would have Millie with her. A little higher, and it would have gone into the cabin. A place where her Millie had always been safe, until now. *Fuck.*

In the elevator, she didn't think anything of her appearance until an older businessman looked her up and down and looked away. Her once-white blouse and black skirt were now a shade of gray from the parking lot. Even her knees were scratched up and bloody. She hadn't felt it at all.

Getting to her floor, she realized she needed a shower and a change of clothes before seeing Win. She would have nothing but questions on this. And Aurora had no answers yet.

Today, her luck was not there at all. First, she was shot at, and then Win was waiting for her in the hallway. Well, not waiting for her. She was watching Xander run up and down the hallway. The kid had some energy.

"What happened to you?" she demanded upon seeing the gray dirt covering Aurora along with her skinned knees.

"Just an incident in the parking lot as I was leaving," Aurora hedged, not wanting Win to know the truth.

Win folded her arms. "Did you get hit by a car?"

"No. Just some crackpot was shooting a gun in the parking lot." Aurora downplayed it.

"At the club? Our club or the other one?" Win asked in disbelief.

The club was where they both felt the most at home. When things got too much in Win's world, she and Aurora went to the club. It had been that way for years. It was the real reason she was always able to drag her friend to pole dancing class—because she got to go home.

"Our club. I left Brandon to deal with it. But I think, um, maybe no pole dancing class this week. I'm thinking of canceling it."

Aurora's hands were shaking as she unlocked her door. Now that

Win knew, she could be nervous about the entire situation. What if Millie had been in the car? She could have been hurt. Until right now she had always felt safe at her club. Would she ever feel safe again?

"You can't let this person make the club seem unsafe. The girls will already feel that enough without you adding to it by canceling activities," Win pointed out as Xander finally went into the apartment. He was completely out of breath.

"You're right, Win. Fuck him." Toeing off her shoes, Aurora kicked them into her apartment.

"That's right, Rora, fuck him. He doesn't get to win!" Win yelled down the hallway.

"Fuck him," Aurora said again, and Aurora's neighbor popped her head out her apartment door and frowned at them.

"Fuck him right, Mrs. Grant?" Win said with a grin, still in her work skirt and matching jacket and heels. Without responding, Mrs. Grant slammed her door shut.

"Can I shower before picking up Millie? If you guys are busy, I can take her now. That's fine. No, I'll just take her now. Get her out of your hair." Aurora turned toward Win's apartment. She needed to do this on her own. Win wouldn't be here forever.

"Shut up, Aurora. Go take a shower." Turing Win went into her apartment, slamming the door before Aurora could respond.

Finally, in her apartment, she stripped at the door. No need to get dirt all over her apartment. In the shower, she let her mind go back to the shooting. Could it have something to do with the letter? And why was Heaven written on the letter?

No answers came before her shower was over. Nor while she dressed. And after she picked up Millie from across the hall, there was no more thinking about it. Win had made her supper and insisted that she spend most of the evening with her and Daniel. It was a nice change from just her and Millie, but it interfered with all the stuff she had wanted to do tonight. But it was worth it for some Win time and Win family time.

CHAPTER
Sixteen

AURORA JUST DROVE OFF.

First, she wandered off, and then she drove off, leaving Declan and the night manager, Tiff, to talk to the cop. Neither of which had the information that was needed. Because she drove off in the only piece of evidence they had.

Declan was pissed that he had backed off the number of men he had working the case. Which meant he had no one in the parking lot today. So far, nothing had ever happened at either the law office or the club. Until this moment, nothing had happened at the club. It was safer than even the law office because the entire staff was watching out for her there. But it hadn't been enough.

On top of that, now he had to worry about Aurora because, until now, he had thought she was safe. Which meant he hadn't had anyone watching out for her except him. And he was stretched so thin he couldn't.

Why wasn't she fazed by being shot at? Sure, she had recognized the sound for what it was, but her reaction was slow. So far, he hadn't been able to dig up much from her past before college. He knew she had more knowledge of unsavory things than anyone he knew.

As he talked to the cop, who didn't seem to take the incident seriously, he realized why Aurora had left. Cops didn't show up at a strip club to help the club or its owner. Just the perceived innocent man. The cop ended up saying nearly when much as he left that they would be looking into it. Which meant nothing would be done about it.

Once the cop was finally gone, Brandon told him he could leave due to the fact that half the customers had already left. Declan didn't even venture back into the club; he just headed to his truck and took off. He called all of his employees to fill them in on what had happened that night. Adding that now everyone would have to be more vigilant at the club and that they needed to start keeping an eye on Aurora. It seemed the shooter was targeting her. Or maybe he had gotten tired of waiting for Gardner and had shot at anyone. And that anyone happened to be Aurora.

As he headed home, he made one last call to Reese, who hadn't been answering her phone. This time, he left her a message to call him immediately, or she was fired.

At his house, he cleaned a little since he never seemed to get a lot done there when he was in the middle of a case. Once the house looked less like a dumping ground and the fridge had been cleared of all the moldy takeout, he turned to paper work.

All the while, he checked the clock, wishing the hands would move faster. He needed it late enough for Aurora's kid to be sleeping.

Last night, he'd been too busy looking at her body to pay any attention to anything in the apartment. The same thing happened this morning. If he didn't know she had a kid, he would still not know now. But he knew where her moles were, and that was way more important.

So far, he hadn't tried to look up information on the kid because it wasn't pertinent to the case. And he wanted to meet the kid, not just know all the facts about it. He wanted to know everything about Aurora's kid, everything about Aurora. But he wanted her to tell him, not some facts here and there from a report. He knew he would have to lie to her about knowing the information, and he was tired of lying to her. Because she always knew.

Getting to his feet, he headed out for the night. It was only nine p.m., but he was tired of waiting to see her. He wanted to see her now —if she let him into the apartment.

Ten minutes into the ride, his phone rang, Reese.

"Where have you been?" he barked into the car since he put it on speaker phone.

"Gardi and I went out for drinks. She got fired today." Reese explained.

"From the club?" He hadn't heard anything about that. Surely, he would have been informed that the girl had been fired—if not by Aurora, by the staff.

"No, from the law firm. No reason, just done," Reese said.

"So, you're friends then?" He didn't want to hear the answer.

"Yeah, she's fun and always so upbeat. Reserved, but once you get to know her, she's a riot. And talk, talk, talk." As she spoke, he could tell Reese was getting to attached.

"Well, don't get too friendly. If she realizes who you are, she won't be happy," Declan pointed out. Hoping his future with Aurora wasn't just as doomed.

"I'm hoping to remain friends with her for a long time," Reese stated in her stubborn voice.

"I wasn't calling you about your awesome new friend, Reese. I was calling because Aurora was shot at outside the club today. You have to be extra vigil around there from here on out, for you and for Gardner," he warned her.

"Is she okay?" There was so much worry in her voice that Declan knew that Gardner wasn't the only one his daughter was getting too attached to.

"Yes, she's fine. They missed her, but she isn't taking it seriously enough. You'll need to keep an eye on her some too."

"Who would shoot at her?"

"I don't know. I'm trying to figure that out. But tomorrow, stop at the house, and I'll get you a gun. I don't know where you will wear it with that tiny get-up you wear at the club. But I want you armed as much as possible."

He tried not to think about the little outfit his kid was in every day. But at least she wasn't stripping. Today, he was happy he had spent years bringing her to the shooting range and knew her way around a gun.

"I can come tonight," Reese said.

Declan wasn't going back home. He was almost at Aurora's. "I won't be there. I have to work."

"Gardi's home and Rex is there. I saw him," Reese pushed.

"Can't I just have a life?" Declan was not telling her where he was going.

"I won't call her mommy," Reese said sarcastically, like she always did when he was dating someone. "Is it a stripper? You have been spending a lot of time at the club."

"Not a stripper," he stated, just a former one.

"You know what? Do the stripper. There isn't one in that place I wouldn't like. Who knew how friendly they were? Last week one even told me a good place to get some bigger tits, and she was just being nice about it. She also told me to keep the tattoos at a minimum if I wanted to start stripping. Though she assured me I would do great if I wanted to give it a try," Reese chatted.

"Not a chance, and I don't really want to hear about your breasts," Declan said.

"They're the second smallest in the club. Only Gardi has smaller. It makes you feel a little inadequate," Reese continued because she knew it irritated him. His daughter didn't have breasts.

"Could you please stop talking?" he demanded.

"We could discuss how my ass is pretty nice, though," Reese said as Declan hung up on her.

If this lasted much longer, he would start to get comfortable talking about his kid's body. He never wanted to be like that. Reese was always bringing it up now. She knew it got to him. She was a little shit.

As he parked on the street, he wondered what Aurora would think about him having a kid who was an adult. She wouldn't have to raise Reese, but she would still be around. Sadly, he was starting to see that they were a lot alike. Both liked to bait him until he got mad or embarrassed.

This time, knocking on her door was way easier. Though he

wondered if she remembered that he had said he was coming tonight. But then again, she never forgot anything, so she would.

When she finally opened the door, he knew she hadn't forgotten at all because she was as naked as the day she was born. Declan didn't notice any kid stuff in her apartment tonight either, or anything about the apartment until they were in the bedroom.

WEDNESDAY'S POLE dancing class wasn't canceled. Win had been right; nobody could make her scared in her own club. Win was even willing to come to class, though she didn't even try this week. Just set up in Aurora's booth with some fancy accounting work from her day job. Aurora gave the class a go for about ten minutes. Her heart wasn't in it, and she was getting enough exercise this week, thanks to the bouncer guarding her girls tonight.

Not even sweating, Aurora slid into the booth across from her best friend. "Does your boss know you work on their numbers at a titty bar, Winter?"

"They don't care as long as they match at the end of the day." Win smiled at her.

"Don't you mean as long as there is a profit?" Aurora asked in confusion.

"I can't make them money. I just count what is there." Win shut her computer.

"Making it is your husband's job." Aurora picked up her newly arrived water glass and took a sip.

"That's right. Everyone's so keyed up around here. The shooting thing has everyone rattled," Win commented as she slid the computer into her bag, work done for the night.

"I know. I hope it settles by the weekend. I'm having a bad month as it is here. Last week's near arrest and now this, the numbers are not going to be good this month," Aurora confided.

Win would understand. She always did.

"I'm sure the second half will be better." Win shrugged, and Aurora relaxed. Win wouldn't be so cavalier about it if it was really going to be a financial disaster.

"I hope so. Are you nervous yet about this weekend?" Aurora was on edge about it, and she wasn't even going.

"Yes, I'm almost completely packed for the second time. Third time!" She made a face of terror.

"Just be you, and they can't help but love you. And if they don't, you will always have me. I love you." Aurora took her hands that had been tapping on the table.

"There's no way you can shake me now, Rora. You'll always be my favorite sister. I mean, there is nobody else who's leftovers I would eat." Win grinned at her.

"I thought when you got married, you would stop that," Aurora said. Win oddly would go into Aurora's apartment for snacks. Which meant she always brought home extra, just in case.

"You have the best food, Aurora. You're always bringing home something from this place. And Friday is steak night. Steak night!" Win raised her voice, and a few tables looked over at them.

"Unless you're getting on stage, Winter, keep your voice down. I need eyes on the tits tonight." Aurora laughed, and so did Win.

"Aurora, I just wanted to make sure you were okay. You didn't participate in class for long tonight. Are you feeling alright?" Gardi West had come up to their table while they laughed.

Aurora stopped laughing. "Gardi, I'm okay. Just not into the class today. See, my friend here is going away for a week, so I wanted to spend some extra time with her."

"Good, I was hoping the thing on Monday wasn't giving you issue," Gardi said in her private school talk.

"Gardi West, this is Win Knight, or McIntosh, I don't know. What is your name, Winter?" She turned to her friend. Aurora couldn't remember that detail from the wedding. Too much had been going on that day, and there was no way she could see her friends as anything but Winter Knight.

"Hello, Gardi. It's Win McIntosh now. I'm trying to shed all the stripper names I can." She laughed, but Gardi didn't get it.

"Sorry, Gardi. Win's name is Winter Rose Knight, which leads to all kinds of stripper names. But she only ever used Starry Night," Aurora told her, always wishing Win hadn't chosen such an awful name when she had so many other great ones.

The kid's eyes went wide at the revelation. "You were a stripper? I thought you were an accountant."

"Kid, I'm a CFO. But I started here. I'm not ashamed of it either."

"But you're awful at class," Gardi let slip, then covered her mouth with her hand.

"That's why I don't do it much. I'm old. Aurora's starting to fail, too." Win pointed right at her.

"You have a kid, and see how you shimmy around that pole," Aurora said to her friend, hating that she couldn't do it anymore.

"How long have you guys been friends?" Gardi asked as the other young waitress came up to the table.

"Over twenty years," Aurora said. "Best thing that ever happened in that shitty reform school was I met Win."

"Awe, you say the sweetest things," Win said.

"Are you ready to go, Gardi?" Reese asked. "I don't want the bouncer to spend his night escorting everyone to their cars."

Aurora looked at the young woman. She was wasting her time delivering drinks to drunk men. For some reason, she was always one step in front of everyone else in the place. Even Aurora sometimes.

"We should go too, Win. While we have a nice group to follow," Aurora said.

With that, the group of four went out to their cars. Aurora now let the employees park close to the door, at least until it felt safe again. Aurora looked around the parking lot and saw nothing, but someone was there. Glancing at Win to see if she felt it, Win kept walking as usual. Win wasn't raised on the streets. She'd just spent a few months there.

Reese was the first to notice anything was up. Her voice was steady and alert as she pointed out, "Aurora, your tires are flat."

Aurora looked at her SUV. Sure enough, all four were completely flat. "Go inside, everyone inside. *Now!*" she yelled at the women.

As one, they turned and hurried back into the club, except Aurora, who was looking at her car tires. The car next to her had no issue. Nor the next one. The third one was flat also. It was Gardi's borrowed red ford SUV. It was the same one she always drove, but not the one she owned based on Aurora's search. Unless her name was Robert David Daws.

"What are you doing?" Declan asked from behind her.

"Seeing if anyone else got their tires slashed." Aurora pointed at the other one. And turned to check the rest of the parking lot.

He grabbed her arm and started to drag her back to the building. "Inside, Carlyle."

"Fuck off, Vincent," she hissed and then got even madder at his reaction. "Fuck off, whoever the fuck you are."

His eyes went wide for a second, but she didn't take the bait. "Are you just waiting to get shot at again, Aurora?"

"They would've already shot me if they were going to. They're long gone," she stated.

"You have no idea what the hell you're talking about." He stared down at her with those gray eyes.

"You have never slashed a tire, cop. When done properly, it takes time for them to go completely flat. If we were going to be shot, it would have been the moment we got close to the vehicle." She shook off his hand.

"And you're such the fucking expert?" he asked.

"Yes, I am. You asshole. You slash the tires and then wait until the person comes out, and then you rob them. I've watched it a hundred times. This was done hours ago." She stomped back into the club, not needing to justify herself to him anymore. He had already gotten more out of her then she should have admitted.

CHAPTER
Eighteen

BACK IN THE CLUB, Win and the two girls were at her booth talking to Brandon, the manager. All had gone back to Aurora's booth, probably because Win felt comfortable there. But Aurora could see that they were all on edge.

Sliding in, all eyes turned to her, but she had no answers. Who would do this and so close to the building? Sure, if they were still parking in the back of the lot, the perpetrator could have done their work unnoticed.

"Gardi's car also had its tires slashed. Everything else looked fine. I don't know why this is happening," she told them what they probably already knew. Gardi looked scared, but Reese looked pissed off. "I'll call someone to take care of the cars, but I'm sure nobody will do anything until tomorrow."

"I already called Daniel. He's coming to get us." Win was still holding her phone. It seemed she was rattled also.

"I can bring Gardi home," Reese said, her eyes darting to the door.

"No, I can call someone. Thank you for offering though, Reese," Gardi argued with a gentle pat on her friend's hand.

"No, Gardi, I'll drive you," Reese insisted, being overbearing on the kid, and Aurora hoped that it worked.

Aurora watched the older of the two concede with a slight nod. It was only then that Aurora told them, "No matter how you two get home, you're off until further notice."

Both turned and looked at her. Reese was the first to recover. "What?"

"You heard me. I can't have my entire staff watching to make sure nothing happens to you two with this shit happening in the parking lot. I'll call you, but I have no fucking idea when," Aurora admitted.

"What?" Gardi asked, just staring at her. The innocence in her green eyes was so cute. The kid had no business being at the club at all.

"You heard me," she shot back at Gardi.

"Aurora, why don't you have them watch Millie at your apartment next week?" Win bumped her shoulder with a sly grin.

Turning to give the stink eye to her best friend, she said, "No."

"It will be perfect. They need jobs, and you need a sitter. Between the two of them, you can have the entire week covered. See if that nanny dream of yours would work. And you wouldn't have to miss any work at all," Win pointed out the logical reason to do it.

"I'll think about it. Maybe I should have you pay for it, Winter. You're the one who is abandoning me." Aurora crossed her arms and leaned back in the booth, looking at the younger girls. Both looked more like baby sitters then waitresses at a strip club.

Gardi perked up at the idea. "I would love to do that for you."

Aurora wondered if there were any ideas she didn't get excited about. She had shown the same excitement to get this job.

"I'm willing, though not quite as excited as her." Reese pointed at Gardi. She, too, it seemed, noticed the other woman's over-excitement about things.

"I saw her last week. She's adorable." Gardi turned to Reese and gushed about the baby.

"Thank you. I picked the cutest one I could find." Aurora smiled. Her kid *was* adorable. Everyone knew that.

"It's set then?" Win asked the table.

"One thing, I need someone every night, in case I get a call to a club in the night. So, one or both. I'll have to buy air mattresses or something." Aurora looked at the two young women.

"My dad has air mattresses. I can bring them. When do we start?" Reese, it seemed, was getting more excited about it.

"Friday. If you're there early enough, I'll take you out to eat," Aurora said, realizing she would have to either feed them or buy groceries for them. This was adding up with every passing minute.

"Take them to that new wood fire grill place. Daniel loves it," Win interrupted.

Aurora shook her head. "I'll take you to the shitty dive Daniel likes."

"Do you guys live by each other?" Gardi asked.

"We live across the hallway from each other. I have an idea." Win looked at the girls. "You guys can camp out at our house, in the living room. Then you can get a little time away. We have a nice TV."

"Winter, you don't know these girls. They will rob you blind," Aurora pointed out as if they were not right across from them.

"Really, that one has bigger diamonds in her ears then I have on my wedding ring, and that one is basically a cop." Win pointed at them, one after another.

"I know, right? And they think I don't notice," Aurora said, ignoring the kids looking at them.

"Like a haze around them." Winter looked at her phone and showed it to Aurora.

"Cops everywhere in this place lately." Getting out of the booth, Aurora looked right at the one by the door, pretending to be a bouncer.

"How do you stand it?" Teasing her, Win followed.

Aurora shrugged at Win. "Friday, I meet you here, and we will take one car into the city. Reese, make sure she gets home. And Gardi, you can pick up your car tomorrow, I'd say sometime after lunch."

"Bye, girls," Win said as they headed for the door.

Once there, Declan pulled her aside. "I stop by tonight, and we will talk."

"No, you work until one in the morning. I won't get up."

"How are you getting around until your SUV is fixed?"

Hello, stinky brown Buick. "Win has a car I can use."

"Will you be here tomorrow?" he questioned, not letting her go, his mere touch making her rethink not letting him come over.

"No, the other club. I have to go. My ride is here," she said, pushing away from him.

"Okay," was all he said, but his eyes were on her until the door closed.

Daniel was in his SUV right by the door, not even in a legal parking spot, but so close to the door that it took three steps to get inside. Win climbed into the front seat, and Aurora sat behind her, pushing Xander to the middle seat. Both kids seemed excited for their late-night adventure. It was after all nine.

"Is trouble brewing in your empire, Aurora?" Daniel asked. Win and Aurora always called her clubs her empire, more appropriate when she had five.

"Seems like stuff keeps happening." She reached out and touched Millie's pajama-clad leg. Then, she let go as the car started moving, and she had to hold on for her life.

"Maybe you need to hire a security team," Daniel suggested.

"I don't have tech company money, Daniel. It should die down in a week," Aurora said, unconvinced as she held tight to the door handle. Having never realized how afraid she was of not being in control in a car.

"Win, I'm using your car tomorrow, and I'm leaving it at the club until after you get back. Then we can shuffle it back. Daniel and I, that is." Aurora closed her eyes.

"I don't know where the keys are still," Win said from the front seat.

"Doesn't matter." Breathe in, breathe out.

"Maybe it will get stolen or shot up." Win's voice hadn't just a little bit of excitement in it.

"With any luck," Aurora agreed, still concentrating on being a passenger and not liking it at all.

"How long has it been since you didn't drive Aurora?" Daniel asked.

"I can't remember. College? No. Before." Aurora had no idea.

"She never rode with me. She's the driver," Win pointed out, and Aurora could tell she looked at her when she said it. But she couldn't open her eyes.

"Shut up, Winter." She breathed deeply, trying to keep herself from puking.

"What's your real name, Aurora?" Winter demanded.

"Shut up, Winter." Aurora put her head between her legs in hopes the world would stop spinning.

"I'll have Daniel drive around until you spill. Or drop you at the door if you tell me." Winter laughed at her discomfort.

"Daniel will be cleaning up the puke if he drives for too much longer." Sitting up, Aurora realized her mistake instantly, and her head went back between her knees.

"Daniel doesn't want to do that," Daniel said from the driver's seat.

"Spill," Winter said.

"Never," Aurora said to the floor.

"Spill," Winter said again.

"We are almost here, Aurora. I'll drop you at the door," Daniel informed her.

"How far?" she asked her new best friend.

"About four blocks," he said as the car slowed for a light.

"Drop me here!" she yelled and undid her seat belt.

She reached for the door handle as Daniel stopped the car, and she practically rolled out of it. On the ground, she kicked the door shut, and Daniel drove away, which left her sitting on the cement sidewalk a few blocks from her place, just trying to breathe. *Trying to gain back control of her life.*

"What was that, Aurora?" Winter asked, sitting down next to her on the sidewalk.

"I have no idea. I don't know if it was car sickness, a panic attack, or both. I have never felt like that before. Ever." Resting her chin on her knees, Aurora looked at the passing cars.

Win hugged her. "I'm sorry I took advantage of you in your weakened state."

"I would have done it to you," Aurora admitted with a chuckle.

"What do you think is happening at the club?" Win asked.

"Something, I have private dicks there all the time. And you invited one into my house," Aurora accused.

"She'll stay at my house. And it's your fault. She isn't of age to serve drinks at your place or be a cop," Win pointed out.

"You saw it too. I think they are all hovering around Gardi, but I don't know why."

"Money?" Win asked as people walked past them. Nobody even looked at them as they did.

"Of course, it's money. She's rolling in money. That's why they're following her, but why is she at my club?" Aurora watched two cars almost hit each other…but didn't.

"Have you talked to your lover about it yet?"

"Fuck you, Winter."

"You think I didn't know. You're so cute. Twenty years, good god, it has been twenty-two years. Longer than those two girls have been alive." Win laughed at how old that made them sound.

"Long enough to drink legally," Aurora pointed out.

"We have been dry so long that if it was human, it can drink now"

"Should we start drinking?" Aurora asked and pointed at a bar behind them, really needing a drink right now.

"Tempting, especially with going to my dad's place this weekend. It would be ironic if I turned back into an alcoholic on his farm." Win chuckled.

"Yeah, and that the only time you don't drink is when you're away from him. See, you can't go there. Stay with me," Aurora begged.

"Going, Rora. But I still love you best. But I am starting to worry about you at the club. I never have before, not at our club, at least." Win hugged her again.

"I am too. I can't get my head around this one," Aurora admitted.

"Are you ready to go home?" Win asked, not getting up until Aurora said she would.

"Yes, I have Millie to put to sleep. Do you think she noticed I fell apart in the car?" She got up and helped Win up.

"I don't think she knew what was happening. She doesn't notice as much as you think she does," Win said as they headed toward their apartments.

"She notices everything." Which was why she had kicked Declan out before the sun came up both nights he had been there. Millie was too smart for her own good.

"Does she notice when you have company in the middle of the night?" Win asked.

Blushing at the words, she said, "You don't even notice that."

"I don't, but I know when you get lucky, and you have gotten lucky lately." Win wrapped an arm around her in comfort.

"Win, you have been spending too much time with that kid around." Aurora laughed and nodded a greeting to the couple coming their way. They weren't anyone she knew, but she tried to be friendly sometimes.

"Aurora, you have been getting fucked." Win laughed, and the middle-aged couple moved a little further away from them.

"That's more like it," Aurora agreed.

She sometimes missed those kid-free days of old when she didn't have to control what she said or did. Maybe she didn't need to change herself. After all, Millie wasn't going to be like all the other girls in school, that was for sure.

Nineteen

ANOTHER DAY of Aurora being at the club and Declan knew it was another day of her being in danger. Yesterday she was at her other club, was she in danger there also? Declan had no one to follow her. She knew every one of them on sight and would know that they were following her.

She had been in danger twice now in so many days, and Aurora's reaction was confusing. She simply didn't believe it. She acted like nothing could touch her at her club. She spent most of her time there, just relaxing like she was in her own living room. Which made sense since she had been involved in the business for half her life.

What he wouldn't give to have seen her on that stage when she was eighteen. Tiff had told him that she worked her way through college right there on that stage. Then she managed the place for years before purchasing it more than seven years ago. The other clubs were for money. This was where she wanted to be. Tiff had also said that she was selling the other clubs to spend more time with her kid. Apparently, Tiff thought that was a stupid move.

With Reese taking Gardi home and the club once again low on customers, Declan and Nick spent an hour or so looking over the parking lot. In the end, they didn't find any clues. But they had new spots that they would be keeping their eyes on in the future.

Tonight, the two women were targeted, but why? Gardi and Aurora had nothing in common. Different backgrounds, different age groups, different friends, nothing that said they could possibly have anything to make them both a target of the same person.

It was well after three in the morning before he and Nick separated, and Declan could finally go home. Aurora had said not to go to her apartment tonight. And she was right. At this time of the night, he was just going there for sex, but he wanted to show her he wanted more. Unfortunately, she had him scheduled such odd hours, making it impossible to do all the paperwork and scheduling that his actual job entailed.

Punching in a familiar number, he listened to it ring until it was answered. "Morning, Honey Bear."

"Can't this wait until morning, dad?" Reese asked sleepily.

"How was the drive home?" He went right into it. When she worked for him, she wasn't his daughter. She was his employee.

"Good, she said she rents a place above the garage. Just lucked out in finding it." Reese chuckled at Gardner's excuse for the fancy house.

"Thanks for taking her home. What did she say about the slashing?" He wondered if she had any clue about what was happening around her.

"Nothing. She couldn't believe that would even happen to her car. That nothing like this had ever happened before. Acted scared." Reese was more awake now, and based on the talking in the background, so was her roommate.

"So, no leads from her?" he surmised, knowing that Gardner wouldn't know anything. She wasn't the sort.

"None, but what about Win? Did you run a background check on her?" Reese asked, knowing he would have already done that.

"Winter Knight McIntosh. They've been friends forever. Both stripped at the club in college. Works for a company downtown now and has been there for years. White collar, no record." That was as much as he had found out about the dark-haired woman.

"Win called me a cop. Then they discussed how the club was

swamped with them. She's onto your operation, but then again, so is Aurora," Reese warned.

"Aurora has called me a cop since the first day," Declan stated, not saying when that first day was.

"I think you have to talk to Aurora. She's definitely not in on it, but she could mess it up really good. It would be good to have her on your side," Reese warned as if she had been doing this for years.

"I'm thinking about it."

Declan wanted to tell her so badly because then he could transition to just a boyfriend. If that's what she wanted. But deep in the back of his mind, he felt she was connected to it. The flat tires said something. It was Gardi and Aurora someone was after.

"Oh, and you can let all your goons have the next week off. Gardi and I are baby-sitting Aurora's kid, twenty-four-seven. Her friend is going out of town, and so is her sitter. Leaving her in a pickle. We'll be downtown in a high-rise apartment. I can keep closer tabs on the woman than anyone else since I'll be living with her." Reese was nearly gloating at the admission. Like she had made it all happen.

He was shocked. Aurora had said nothing about it. "When was that decided?"

"She was going to lay us off until whatever this is blows over, but Win told her to have us babysit instead. Gardi was so excited about it. But she does get excited about everything. We are spending the nights in Win's apartment. She lives across the hallway. Simple solution." Reese was just a fountain of information tonight.

"Do you have any more information?" Declan asked as he turned his car toward the city.

"No, I think that's all. Oh, except she knows I'm not twenty-one," Reese said.

"You told her?" Declan demanded, as if her getting fired from the club wouldn't be the best thing to happen to him as a father.

"No, she was telling her friend. You should see them together. I really like these people," Reese said and then hung up on him.

As Declan drove to the city, he decided he would have to figure out how to get his guys in the apartment building in two days. Downtown with all its people and movement. And a top-floor apartment. Thank god Reese was going to be in the apartment with Gardner for the week because Declan knew it would be hard to keep her safe without someone on the inside.

He would also have someone outside the building, just in case. Just because they weren't going anywhere didn't mean they weren't suddenly sitting ducks. His job was to keep Gardner safe, and he was going to do it. With any luck, he would be able to spend the night in the building himself. He liked it there.

CHAPTER
Twenty

IT WAS Friday at four in the afternoon. Aurora was already missing Win, and she had probably not even left yet. But Aurora was across town picking up Millie from Penny's place since Daniel couldn't today. His ex was picking up Xander for the week.

Then it was back to the club to pick up the girls since they didn't want to leave their cars on the street all week. Aurora was glad to be back in the driver's seat, never again with the passenger thing. She was back in control of her life.

Yesterday, Daniel had taken Millie to Penny's in the morning so Aurora could go to the club and get the cars fixed. Win's car still stunk, so she left the windows open when she parked it at the club. They were probably still open. It didn't matter. By the time Win got back, it would be gone. If Aurora knew anything, it was how to get rid of cars. If Win wanted a car, she would need a new one anyway.

Yesterday, Aurora had gotten another extortion letter addressed only to Carlyle. This time, it was more threatening, but in a general way. No specifics. This time, the blackmailer asked for $50,000 to be delivered the same way as before, on Wednesday. The postmark was from Tuesday, which meant whoever sent it had no concept of how the mail service operated.

The drop day happened to be the same day the tires had been slashed. Aurora wondered if maybe they were connected. But she hadn't thought much of it since tire slashing didn't feel in the same category as extortion.

Pulling into the club, she parked where the employees were supposed to park. Now they parked as close to the door as possible, so there was plenty of open space out here. Gardi's car was already parked in the far spot, but she wasn't in it. Looking around, Aurora wondered where the girls were. She was starting to see that this was a bad idea.

Leaving the car running, she got out of the SUV, went over to Gardi's, and checked inside. Nothing. No luggage, no garbage, no nothing. Looking around the lot, she had the familiar sense of being watched. Dismissing it as Declan's operation, she leaned against the car and watched for their arrival.

This morning, she went over the surveillance video from Wednesday and found that her tire had been slashed close to five in the afternoon, her usual leaving time. As she had suspected, the event was over long before they went outside after eight. The culprit was fully covered, so she had no way of knowing anything about him or her. The cost of eight new tires was cheap compared to calling the cops.

Aurora had been avoiding Declan for two days now. Maybe it was the reason she didn't slip into the club and show off her daughter. *Declan*. He had to know she had a kid. Everyone who worked for her knew about Millie. Two nights in a row, he had worked late, and today he was off. So he shouldn't be at the club, but she wasn't going in there anyway.

If she went in with Millie, she wouldn't get out of there for an hour or more. Besides, the last thing her customers wanted to see was the strippers with a baby. Many were there to get away from family-like scenes like that. So, she stayed out.

Looking at her club and the cars in front, she remembered back to Wednesday night when she had called Declan by his last name, and he hadn't reacted. It had thrown her off more than she had imagined it would. In the back of her mind, she knew it wasn't his actual name, but seeing the proof was different. He had a tiny moment of confusion when she called him that. People don't hesitate with real names. Now she had no idea who she was sleeping with, and she hated that.

Still leaning against the SUV, she saw Reese's SUV drive into the parking lot. Another liar there. Reese Nicholas was actually Reese Chamberlain, an almost twenty-one-year-old college student who should know better than to drive a car registered in her name when working undercover. At least Gardi had been smart enough to borrow other people's cars. So far, she'd had four different ones and not one registered to her.

When Reese stopped, Aurora met them at the back end to help load up their stuff. And stuff they had, from sleeping bags and air mattresses to six bags of stuff. Aurora didn't think she had that much stuff when she was twenty. In fact, she knew she didn't have that much stuff. She had two bags of clothes, that was all. Enough that she could carry it all easily, and she did on many occasions.

Gardi reached into the back seat and happily produced two paper bags. "We bought food."

"No alcohol, right? Or drugs?" Aurora eyed the bags wearily.

"No, never," Gardi said. She didn't lie much, just sometimes, and she was bad at it. This was not one of those times.

"Okay," Aurora said, taking one of the bags from the younger woman.

The unmistakable pop of a gunshot blasted through the parking lot.

The sound was Deja vu for Aurora, same SUV, same area of the lot. No Declan this time. Dropping the bags, she grabbed both young women's clothes, pulling them to the ground. Pushing them away from the back end of the SUV, she had no idea how to get to Millie, who was trapped in her car seat. To her surprise, it was Reese who bravely climbed into the vehicle. Within minutes, she had freed the baby and had her on the floorboards of the car.

In the midst of the chaos, more shots were fired in their direction. Keeping between the gunman and Gardi, she felt the old fear course through her body. This was the same fucking thing she had left behind at fourteen. She swore she would never be this scared again—scared of dying, scared for her daughter, and scared for the others around her.

Shoving Gardi deeper into the gravel as if that would protect her,

Aurora jumped to her feet to take her fucking life back. The bastard had done enough damage to her business in the last week. Now it was her turn to tell him to fuck off.

Getting to her feet, she saw him instantly. He was walking toward her and was holding a gun. Waving a gun was more like it. He was around sixty with gray hair and dark eyes, just a middle-aged man in khakis and a green polo shirt. His eyes were pinned on her, and he had the perfect shot. But he didn't take it. He looked behind her, and his eyes went dark. Raising the gun, she watched him pull the trigger.

Or almost pull the trigger. Instead, she heard a pop but watched him tumble backward with a surprised look on his face. Down he went, and he didn't move. Looking around, she saw a man with a gun running toward her.

A man she recognized. She'd had him kicked out of her club weeks before for lingering and touching her waitresses. Realization hit hard. He was another cop, or cop used-to-be.

"Can I get the fuck out of here? I'll take the girl," she called to him, pointing to her SUV, where both girls were still hiding.

He slowed and looked at her. "Go," he said, not questioning what girl or where she would go. Just waved her off.

Taking one last look at the guy on the ground, who was not moving, she knew she had never seen him before. And she would never see him again. That she also knew. Spinning, she yelled at the girls to get in the SUV. She hurried to the driver's seat. Aurora glanced at Gardi as she climbed shakily into the back seat. Reese and Millie were still on the floor but getting up now as another joined them. So far, Millie had taken it all in but hadn't cried. A Carlyle through and through.

Slipping into the driver's seat, she saw Declan's guy on the phone. He kicked the downed guy as he talked, as if making sure he was dead. Making sure the guy didn't move, Aurora waited for a second longer before peeling out of the lot. She was blocks away before she saw the cop lights coming down the road toward her club. *Another shitty night at the club, another shitty Friday night at the club.*

"Anyone have any idea what that was?" she asked the backseat as she watched Reese putting Millie in her car seat.

Gardi was numbly staring out the window, her answer barely audible. "No."

"Nope," Reese lied as she calmly snapped the car seat straps together.

Aurora felt that they were both lying right now but had no idea about what part of the night. And she had no energy to make them talk. Things were getting worse.

CHAPTER

Twenty~One

NICK'S CALL sent chills through Declan's entire body. Aurora, Reese, and Gardner had been shot at by some guy. Nobody was hurt, and Nick had let Aurora leave with the women. The cops were pissed. The guy was dead, but the most important thing about it was that the women were all safe.

Pulling into the club parking lot, he saw it was nearly empty of cars except for cop cars. Of which there were twelve. Getting out of his truck, he walked right to Nick, who was talking with an officer who appeared to be in charge. It wasn't the officer who had been there the night Aurora had been shot at.

"What the hell happened?" Declan asked Nick.

"I was here already because Reese said they were meeting up at four at the club. Rex was tailing them to the grocery store. Aurora came first and wandered around for a bit, then just waited. Once the girls arrived, they moved all the stuff to Aurora's vehicle. On the last load, this guy came out of nowhere and started shooting at them. I don't know who he was trying for, maybe any of them. All of them," Nick explained, pointing to the grocery bags with their contents scattered across the parking lot.

"Aurora saw me and recognized me. I think the jig is up with her. I assume you know where they went? Because I didn't ask. I really don't think she would have told me anyway." Nick was still looking around the lot as if something else might happen. Which it might, this place was a hotbed of danger.

"Yes, I know." Declan knew he had to tell her now. He should have told her before. Now it might be too late.

It took over two hours for the cops to process the scene and the body. To Declan's surprise, the cops were saying that it was a mugging outside a strip club. Unfortunate, but it happened. The guy was a known sex offender who had slipped through the cops' hands many times over the years. He had his wallet on him, and the gun was even registered to the man.

Even more interesting, the dead man had been a lawyer from the law firm that Gardner had worked for until just last week. Not that he had filled in the cops; there didn't need to be a spotlight on Gardner. The shooter wasn't the lawyer she had worked for, just another guy from the same office. It couldn't be a coincidence even though Gardner hadn't done anything but filing while she worked there, as far as he knew.

This was just a sloppy attempted murder that want wrong. But maybe only because they were watching Gardner Westmoreland. Was Aurora alive today because of her? Why would someone connected to Garner be targeting Aurora?

He decided to go into the city to stay with Aurora or at least keep the girls safe. He sent a text to Reese in case she could talk. But she didn't text back right away, and he started off on the half an hour drive.

His mind was playing over everything that could have gone wrong today. The guy could have killed them all: his client, his daughter, and the woman he was falling for. Not to mention the baby in the car at the time. The thought of losing them all gave him chills.

A few blocks from the apartment building, he finally started to get texts. Quite a few of them. Once parked, he pulled out his phone to look at who was so persistent. They were all from Reese.

REESE: We are all okay.

REESE: All are shook up, Aurora's pissed.

REESE: Aurora kicked us into Win's apartment already. Gardi is still a little scared but excited for the sleep over.

REESE: Got to see the baby, cute.

The last one was accompanied by a picture of Reese cheek-to-cheek with a baby. Declan dropped his phone as if it burned him. Then, he carefully picked it up again. Looking at the picture closely, he stared at his daughter, who was cheek-to-cheek with his other daughter. There was no way the baby was not his. Reese looked exactly the same when she was a baby, except Aurora's baby also had his eyes.

He didn't have to calculate anything. He had no idea how old the baby was. But she was born nine months after their three-day affair in November.

Slamming his hand into the steering wheel, he was pissed at himself. He had lied to her about who he was and had left her with no way to contact him. As of now, he had missed his daughter's first year and even longer with her mom. All because he thought that he could do casual and walk away. Except he couldn't get the woman out of his mind.

Getting out of the truck, he had to figure out what to say to her, and he only had twenty-five floors to do it. By the time he got there, he hadn't figured it out yet. Glancing at Apartment 2505, the one with his kid and Gardner in it, he breathed a sigh of relief. He needed to talk to Aurora alone. Turning to 2515, Declan rang the doorbell.

Just when he thought that she wasn't going to answer, she swung the door open and demanded, "Who the fuck are you?"

"Can I come in?" He didn't want to do this in the hallway, which would most likely bring out Reese and Gardner.

"I don't let people I don't know into my apartment," she hissed.

Tonight, she was wearing black leggings and a yellow blouse. Declan liked her better when she answered the door naked.

"Let me in, and I'll tell you." He wasn't going to let her make him raise his voice and draw any more attention to them.

"Fuck you," she said and slammed the door shut.

Catching it with his foot, it bounced back at her, but she was already walking away from him. Following her into the apartment, he closed the door behind him. She stopped mid-stride, turned to him, crossed her arms with a huff, and stared at him.

"Do you really think that any explanation you give will make me say that it was okay to put my kid in danger?" Her voice didn't raise, but her temper was high enough.

"You think I planned what happened?"

"I have no fucking idea. You have been lying to me from the moment I met you." She held her voice steady.

He was silent as she stared at him. He had no comment. He had been lying to her. Since the very beginning. He should have talked to her when Gardner started working at the strip club. Explained every-thing instead of simply getting a job there. But he couldn't change that now.

"Get out before I call the cops." Her voice was chilly. It was a tone that he had never heard before.

"You will never call the cops." He called her bluff. "You hate cops."

"Bullshit! I don't call the cops to my business. I'll call them here. Mr. Fucking Chamberlain. Didn't think I would connect the dots, did you?" she spit out at him.

"How did you figure it out?" he asked, impressed. He knew she knew he was not a Vincent, but to actually get the name right. She was a cunning one.

"One word of advice: don't hire family, and don't let them use their own cars," she hissed.

Reese had been her connection. "How did you know she was my relative?"

"You were too familiar with her. You haven't learned to stay distant. You're fucking shit at family crime. And all your goons, fuck, I have been trying to get rid of them for over a month." She shook her head.

He folded his arms. "You have it all figured out?"

"Who is Gardi? And what's she doing at my club?" Her voice was still hard.

"I don't know why she was at your club. Who is Paul King?" He had questions of his own. Maybe she had the answers.

"No fucking idea. A dead guy, I assume. I've never seen him before." She dismissed the idea of her being in danger, like always.

"Then why does he want you dead?" He wanted to know, needed to know the answer.

"He doesn't. He had the opportunity to shoot me. He wanted Gardi," she said, her head turned again away from him.

"You can't know that," he argued.

"Fuck I can, you bastard! I stood right in front of him, and he looked past me at her!" she yelled.

His heart had stopped at her words. "What were you doing standing in front of him?" Why was she so willing to put herself in danger?

"Showing him that he can't fucking scare me. I'm not scared of a fucking gun." Her words were hard and controlled.

"You should be." He didn't understand how she could rationalize the danger she had put herself in today. On purpose, it seemed.

"Fuck you." Turning, she walked away from him, going toward her bedroom.

Standing in the middle of her apartment alone, he looked around like he hadn't in all the times he had been here before. Comfortable furniture in shades of green was dotted with things for her baby. There was a high chair in the kitchen, a car seat by the door, and a few toys on the floor.

Walking out of the back of the apartment, she was carrying a baby, his baby. The child was in pink pajamas, and her dark hair was pulled into a tiny ponytail on the top of her head. She was smiling and happily tapping her still pissed-off mom's cheeks.

"You may leave now. You can take your kid if you want. I can take care of the other one more than you can," she stated calmly.

"Stop Aurora." He pulled her into his arms, the baby between them. "Just listen to me, please."

"Talk away. I don't know if I'll listen to you or not." She hugged the baby closer to her and put her hand protectively on the back of her head.

"My name is Declan Chamberlain. I was hired by Royal Westmoreland to watch his daughter. To let her spread her wings, but to keep an eye on her. It seems working at a strip club was on her bucket list. I've been turning over men, keeping one on the inside. I don't know why she's at the club."

"What about your underage kid?" she asked.

"She got herself hired; thank you for hiring her. She's supposed to be in college during the day. And she's only a month from being twenty-one." He leaned against the back of her couch, watching her cuddle the baby.

"Why didn't you just talk to me? I would have allowed you inside, no issue." She told him what he had figured out over the last month.

He wished he had done just that. "Gardner doesn't know we are following her."

She shook her head. "Gardner?"

"She comes from enough money that you don't get picked on for your name," he admitted, though it seemed the name hadn't rung a bell with Aurora.

"Who was Paul King?" She brought his name back into it because she remembered everything.

"A lawyer downtown that she was also working for until last Friday." His eyes were on the baby girl, who snuggled closer to her mom like he wanted to.

"Rich enough to have two jobs?" she asked in disbelief.

"I don't know what she was really doing. Cops are calling his death a mugging, and they won't spend any time on it. He was a sex offender, and they don't want to look too deeply into it."

Aurora paused. "Do you think he did anything to her?"

"I didn't get the impression she knew him before she started at his office." He hoped he was right. He didn't want to think of any harm coming to Gardner, not only because he was getting paid to keep her safe.

"Any connection from the dad or the mom to the guy?"

"Nothing like that that I'm aware of."

She went to the table where her briefcase was. "But you're shitty at your job, so I'll look."

"I'm not bad at my job," he argued.

"You haven't figured this out in a month. Whatever your name is." Pulling the laptop from the bag, she nearly dropped it since she was still holding the baby.

Catching it before it slipped from her grasp, Declan handed it to her so she could grab it easily. "Declan, still."

"Who cares."

Dismissing him, she grabbed her computer from him and walked into the living room to sit on the couch. Crossing her legs in front of her, she put the baby in the hole that was created and balanced the laptop on her legs. He could tell she had done this many times before. As she typed, the baby tapped on the edge of the computer.

"What is her name?" Without waiting for an invitation, he sat down on the other end of the couch. Reached out his hand to touch her, his daughter, missing all the time he had missed in her life.

Slapping his hand away, she said, "Millicent Winter."

"After your friend?" Declan tried again and was slapped again.

Aurora was busy on the computer. Busy enough that she missed him touching Millicent's hand. Millicent pulled away from him with a feisty look she had inherited straight from her mom. A few more tapes and Aurora said, "King liked young girls. Gardi is ten years too old for him."

"How do you know?" He finally looked at the screen in front of her. Somehow, she had his complete rap sheet.

"Never mind how I know." She slapped his hand away again from her daughter.

"I don't even have access to that."

"You should, it's very useful," she said smugly.

He watched as she typed Gardner's father's name into the search engine. "You think Royal Westmoreland has a record?"

"Probably not, but rich guys love to fuck little kids."

He was taken aback at her words. "How do you know that?"

"Some moms like to have their kids fuck rich men." She gave him a weary look as she pulled her daughter tighter into her arms.

"What?" he asked, wondering if he had heard her wrong but knowing he hadn't.

"Westmoreland has nothing on his sheet. But he also has enough money not to. But no way would his daughter be involved. So why would he want her dead?" Her eyes were staring out the balcony doors at the city lights, probably trying to solve the case with just that information.

"Not as easy as you thought it would be." He also looked out the window at the city lights. His mind was still on her calm statement about being raped as a child. As if it happened to everyone, but maybe it did happen to everyone she knew.

"I would have it solved already if you had just told me when she started working for me." Her cockiness had returned, and the past was back where she kept it, in the past.

So far, she hadn't kicked him out, and she seemed over her anger at him already. But there was more to come because he hadn't told her everything. Yet.

CHAPTER
Twenty~Two

SLAPPING his hand away from her baby, Aurora looked at the computer again. Years before, she had dated a man for a few months who had given her all the tools she would need to do proper background checks on people. She had been able to weed out some very bad people using that information in her clubs.

But tonight, she couldn't go deep enough to make a connection between the two men and the woman one of them was trying to kill. There was one; she just couldn't see it.

Clapping the baby's hands together while she thought, she heard her phone in the bedroom. She must have left it there after she changed when she got home. Moving the computer to go get it, Declan's hand held her back.

Shrugging, she let him do the task of getting her phone. There was nothing he could destroy on her phone. Watching him leave the room, she couldn't help but admire his lying ass. It looked good in those jeans.

Aurora closed her eyes and channeled her inner Sylvia Carlyle, the master criminal. What would Sylvia be up to in this triangle? Of course, Sylvia was a scammer, so she would be scamming someone.

Westmoreland or King? Westmoreland was obvious, so Sylvia would go the other way.

Opening her eyes, she searched the internet for something. Looking at the images the search brought up, she thought about what she was seeing. But it was still nothing that made any sense, except that in the right clothes, Gardner Westmoreland could make a statement at a charity gala. She was a knockout when not slumming at a strip club. And she had probably been invited to so many galas she had an entire section of her closet for dresses, or maybe an entire room based on who her daddy was.

"Here." Declan gave her the phone and sat back down, even closer than before.

Trying to ignore him completely, she looked at the phone and saw that Win had called and texted, and she had missed it. Looking at the text, she saw an almost empty bottle of liquor. Hitting the call button, she looked back at the pictures.

"What is this picture of?" Aurora asked, not accusing. If Win chose to drink, that was on her.

"I found it in my room." Win sounded so proud of her teenage self's ability to hide things.

Aurora wasn't as proud. Win was still a recovering alcoholic, and being at her dad's was enough to knock her off the wagon. Hopefully, Daniel was doing his job of keeping the woman safe.

"Did you drink it?" Aurora asked tentatively.

"No, and Daniel won't. He says it'll be bad after all these years. But I still want to know how much water is in it." Win laughed at her young self.

"Would you have put water in it if you were hiding it in your room?" Aurora knew that Win could be devious if need be, but she didn't know how far back that went.

Win seemed to think for a moment, "I would have added the water before taking the entire bottle. I'm sure it's all water, but why keep it then?"

"Are you sleeping in your former room?" Aurora changed the subject, hoping to get Win's mind off the past and that bottle.

"Oh yeah. They offered a spare room, but no way."

"You're having sex in your teenage bedroom." Aurora surmised. There was no way she and Daniel were not. They may have been back from their honeymoon for months, but they were still on it.

"You bet I am," Win said in a low voice, probably looking at her man with dirty thoughts in her mind.

"Good job. Did you get my spoon?"

"Not yet. I know which one I'm taking. We just have to wait for night to take it."

"You're thinking of me!"

"I am. How are things at the club?" This time, Win changed the subject.

"Nothing big," Aurora lied. If she told Win about the shooting, she would come home. As much as she didn't want her to go, she didn't want to be the reason she left early.

Win exhaled. "Good, I was worried."

"Are you going to find any drugs in your room?"

"No, I wouldn't leave those behind. Alcohol was easy to get, drugs, not so much."

"Did you at least get twenty birthday presents today? And, of course, Christmas one? A Car?" Aurora shut her computer and turned the baby to her.

"No, I told them not to. We did talk tonight, just me and dad. I think he's starting to understand what actually happened all those years ago."

Aurora tickled the baby and asked, "Did you tell him everything, Winter?"

"Most of it," her friend hedged. Win had a hard time with tough personal conversations.

"He needs to know all of it." She tickled her baby again, and Millie giggled.

"I will, in my own time."

"Graduation?" was all Aurora asked. It was one word that said everything. It was the day Win had nearly died at her own hands because her father had let her down. Not for the first time, but for the last.

"Not yet," Win admitted with a sigh.

"Did you want me to? I'm more than willing." Aurora looked at her perfect baby and pulled her in for a hug.

"I can do it," Win argued, though even she sounded unconvinced of her abilities.

"Oh, Miss I-Don't-Talk is going to talk to her dad? I call your bluff. Tell him to call me. I'll even tone it down for him," Aurora promised. It had been a speech she had practiced over and over in her mind over the years. So far, she hadn't been unable to hit the man over the head at the end. But she would try.

"You won't," Win accused.

"Your right, I was there, he wasn't." Aurora restrained from swearing.

"Kiss Millie for me. She's keeping your mouth in check." Win laughed.

"She is. Millie says hi, Winter." Aurora waved the baby's hand at the phone, though Win wouldn't see it.

"Hey, Millie girl," Win's said in a sing-song voice.

"Millie says to just sit down and talk to them. Show them the shitty tattoos." Aurora said far more seriously.

"I have a week," Win hedged, and Aurora let it go. They would talk again by the time the week was out. She would push again then. "I have to go. Call you again soon."

"I'll call if I miss you too much. Or those girls rob you blind." Aurora was happy that Win laughed at her joke.

Hanging up the phone, Aurora set it on the arm of the couch and turned her complete focus to her baby girl. Win might be gone, but Millie was here. And, of course, the guy who was just sitting watching her.

Turning her to face Millie, she played peek-a-boo for a while as Declan just watched her. "Millie girl, isn't that guy super annoying? And a liar. A big fat liar, and we don't like liars. Or cops."

"Can I defend myself? Millie might like me if you don't turn her against me." He reached for her, but a look from Aurora stopped him.

"No, she already doesn't like you. She's a very good judge of character." She clapped the baby's hands together again.

"I think she'll go to anyone who wants to hold her." The baby's little gray eyes were on him. She was smiling now.

"Nope, the smile hides her anger at you. She thinks you're an ass." Aurora tickled her again and made her laugh.

"What does she need to know to maybe like me again? I'm a former cop who has a private investigating firm now. Twice divorce with one kid." His eyes were on his other kid. There was no denying it.

"I knew you were a cop." Aurora felt justified. She had been right and held the baby's arms in a victory stance.

"Sorry, I said I wasn't. But I wasn't anymore." He reached over and touched Aurora's leg. This time, she didn't give him the stink eye, so he left it.

"Not forgiven. So now that King is dead, are you done?" She set the baby back down in the space her legs still made as she sat cross-legged.

"No, we are just supposed to make sure she's okay. No end date." He was starting to hate the no-end-in-sight case. It was starting to be a hindrance to what he really wanted, Aurora.

"Well, I do believe that I'm firing all of you," Aurora said, though she had already basically fired the two. The only one left was Declan. So, it would be easy to do right now, except she didn't for some reason.

"You're not losing me that easily. Someone tried to kill you tonight." Millie touched his hand on her mom's leg.

"You mean her, Westmoreland." Aurora pointed at the door to the hallway.

"I think that you were the target. She has no enemies," he stated because the kid was the most innocent person he had ever met.

"I have no enemies. Everyone loves me. She's some sort of a heiress. Heiresses are always being kidnapped, murdered, etcetera." She huffed.

"You're grasping at straws." His eyes were on his daughter's hand on his, all soft and warm and wet.

"I'm not. This is all on her. Why she's in my club, I have no idea. But I have to put my daughter to bed. You can leave." She dismissed him.

"I'm not leaving. Gardner is here for a week, so this week, I'm following you. You're in danger," he said again as if she should be worried.

"You can go sleep at Win's place. Send Gardner over here. Cops can sleep with their fleas." She walked out of the room with her baby in her arms and her computer.

Instead of going into Millie's room, she went into her own room. The baby was nowhere near tired, but Aurora needed to be away from Declan. When he was too close, she had a hard time thinking, and he was too close when they were in the same room. She had a lot of information to process about the man. Was he still lying to her? Yes, he was, about something.

Closing the bedroom door, she set the baby near the toy basket and sat on the floor, leaning against her bed. Opening the computer again, she typed in his name to see what she could find on the man who was slowly taking over her life. By the time she had read everything she could about him, she knew he hadn't lied to her tonight. That didn't forgive him for everything he had lied about over the past month.

Next, she checked Reese Chamberlain. She was clean except for a speeding ticket last year. She was enrolled at the same college Aurora and Win had attended years before. Nothing interesting, not that Aurora had expected there to be anything.

Millie handed her a red block as she entered Gardner Westmoreland into the search. Spinning the block in her hand, she read more about the kid. Graduated from a private school, went to a private college, and graduated with a degree in education. No criminal record, no tickets, clean as she looks. But Aurora hadn't expected anything from her. She was a princess.

Millie grabbed the block from her as she turned the computer away from her daughter. Typing in Heaven and not Aurora, she was shocked by what she found. Arrest after arrest for years, and as recent as last summer. From selling drugs to solicitation. Someone was using her identity, the one she had left behind a lifetime ago.

Looking back at the beginning, she saw that nothing from her youth was actually on the record. *Thank you for the expunging of minor records.* But since the age of thirty, the rap sheet was packed. There was even an arrest warrant out for her. Someone was using her identity, and Aurora didn't have to think too hard to come up with a name.

Typing in Debbie Carlyle, she was not at all surprised the woman hadn't been arrested in years. Seven years. Of course, her own mother would have taken her identity. She had done it before. Aurora's identity was so wrapped up with her mom that she had gotten a new social security number when she got a new name.

Closing her computer and setting it aside, she took her baby in her arms. Rocking her, Aurora wondered what she should do about the identity thing. It really wasn't hers anymore, and she didn't want it back. But she really wanted her mom in prison, and by the looks of her crimes, that was where she deserved to be.

Rocking Millie to sleep, she tried to forget that her mom was the worst person in the world. Only her mom would steal her daughter's identity twice in one lifetime. Who else had she stolen over the years? There had to be dozens of people who lost everything because of her. Or maybe not everything. Debbie wasn't that good, but what she lacked in brains, she made up for in meanness.

Closing her eyes, she wondered if her mom had become as good at crime as her grandma had been. Sylvia was the one in charge of every criminal act they had ever done. Debbie never had the brains, and Sylvia would always point that out. Aurora was in charge when Sylvia was out or arrested, never Debbie. In fact, when Debbie did try her hand at something, Aurora was always nervous that it would go south —because it usually did.

Getting up off the floor, she walked across the hallway to Millie's room and put her down in her white crib that had nothing but pink bedding in it. Even Aurora knew that the baby was going to revolt one day and wear other colors, but until then, she was going to do what she wanted.

Just looking at her dark-haired baby sleeping, she wondered how her own mother could have done everything she had done to her own baby. All Aurora wanted to do was protect her daughter from the world, and she had no idea what it would be like not to care about her.

Not just her baby but others also. For now, she had to protect Gardner from whoever was trying to kill her and to find out why. It had been over an hour since she had left Declan in her living room, and she hoped he had left. She was fine without him.

Instead, he was sitting comfortably on the couch watching TV when she came out of the back bedroom. All relaxed and not gone from her apartment.

"Can you get out of my apartment?" she demanded of him.

Declan's eyes didn't leave the TV. "Nope, you're in danger, and I'm going to protect you."

"I don't need you." She informed him because she didn't need anyone.

"But you want me." He finally pulled his eyes off the TV screen and shut it off with the remote.

"Fuck you," she hissed because it was true. She wanted him.

"Okay," he said, getting up and walking toward the bedroom, pulling his shirt off as he went.

"Not what I meant, whoever you are." She followed him, not yelling in case she woke the baby. "Get out of my apartment."

"No, I have now been invited to stay." His shirt was off, and he was losing his pants just as quickly.

"That was not an invitation, you asshole." Her mouth went dry as his boxers hit the floor. He was as turned on as she was.

"Felt like an invitation to me." He walked past her and shut the door. "Because I want to fuck you, Aurora."

As his arms went around her, she tried to make her body fight his off, but she wanted him there. Damn her for wanting him there.

DECLAN WOKE up alone in a panic, thinking Aurora had bolted, probably taking the kid with her. He wouldn't put it past her, just as he knew he wouldn't be able to find her if she left. Her ability to keep him on his toes was starting to be legendary.

One look at the clock said it was almost seven, and the sun had come up long ago. Throwing on his pants, he left the bedroom to find her. She could be anywhere. He was already worried about her and the baby being alone.

Stopping short in the kitchen because he found her, a spatula in hand, an eyebrow quirked at him. The food was already being consumed by Gardner and Reese, who were seated on either side of the high chair.

He must have made too much noise because both turned to look at him. Today, they were dressed in the same attire Reese wore on days she wasn't leaving the house: lounge pants and oversized t-shirts. Neither said anything as he stood tongue-tied as to how to explain why he had been in Aurora's apartment—in her bedroom.

"Ladies, you know Declan from the club." Aurora was already decked out in a gray skirt and teal blouse with a devilish smirk as she pointed a spatula at him.

"Morning, Declan." The smirk on his kid's mouth could only be matched by the one on his lover's.

Gardner's focus was on feeding the baby beside her. He was happy the princess was there for his infant daughter because his adult daughter wasn't as nurturing. Which was all his fault, but he liked her rough-and-tumble nature and couldn't see her being a baby person.

Millie didn't notice or care that he was there because all her focus was on the eggs on her plate and the ones being hand-fed to her. She was still dressed in the pink pajamas from the night before, but they were covered in egg and what he assumed was yogurt.

"Good morning." He tried to act like this was normal and that he was always there.

It was only then that Gardner looked up from spooning the eggs into Millie's mouth and noticed him. Doing a double take before turning back to the baby, she didn't say anything.

Walking past the table, he went for the coffee pot on the counter. Filling his cup, he said, "So you two are staying here with Millie. I'll go with Aurora to her other club today. Because I have to work."

He added the last line for Gardner alone. If she realized that they were guarding her, she would probably tell her dad, and Declan would get fired. The next team might not be as concerned for her safety as he was.

"No, you have the day off. I'll just go alone. Like usual," Aurora said as she cracked another egg into her pan.

"You'd think I would remember my shift better than you. And I think that after last night, you need someone watching over you," he said through gritted teeth.

"I *think* you are overreacting."

Brushing her brown hair behind her back, Gardi looked up from the baby. "Please take him, Aurora. It is dangerous out there. So far, we don't know who that was yesterday. I'd feel better if you had Declan watching out for you, even if it's his day off."

"I'll be okay, Gardi. One crazy person does not make my clubs dangerous. One isolated incident won't change that." Aurora assured her, dodging Declan from touching her on his way back to the table.

Before he sat down with his cup, he touched Millie on the head, which he could tell bothered the shit out of Aurora. *You don't just touch her kid, ever.* He could see in her eyes. But he was going to touch his kid if he wanted. Because he had missed a lot of her life and he wanted any connection he could get,

"No argument, Aurora. I'll drive."

"Fuck, no, I drive," her voice cracked as she said it before she finished with a cough. Had he found a weakness in the woman? How could it be driving with everything else?

"Fine, you can drive." Declan smiled. He knew he had won the argument when she slammed a plate of eggs down in front of him. He was surprised the plate didn't break.

Beside him, Reese gave him a knowing look, one that said she knew what was going on. He ignored it. It was bad enough that he had conversations about breasts with her lately. She wasn't having one about sex, and his sex life was off-limits.

Twenty-Four

THE MOMENT the girls were done eating, Aurora kicked them back to Win's apartment. She didn't need them around when she was home with her baby. This was her time with Millie. It wasn't so easy to get rid of Declan. He opted to take a shower since she was ignoring him anyway.

Trying not to picture him naked in her shower and failing, she sat on the floor with Millie and helped her stack her blocks. This was her favorite time with her, when they were alone and had all morning to do nothing but what the little girl wanted to do. Before long, the liar joined them, and Millie decided the man was okay in her book and started to hand him her blocks.

Declan, for his part, played with the girl and fully engaged with her. But, of course, he had a kid, so this was nothing new for him—even if his kid was almost twenty-one.

"Your kid sure enjoyed seeing you this morning," Aurora said, remembering the smirk on Reese's face.

"I hadn't realized you had invited them over so early."

"They are my guests. If you didn't want your kid to see what you're up to, you should have left last night," she said, so maybe she had invited the girls over for that exact reason—because he deserved it.

"I don't think she really cares what I do," was his only response.

"Oh, she cares. But I'm the kind of person everyone loves, so she doesn't mind," Aurora pointed out. "Your kid is old. How old are you?"

Smirking as he watched the baby crawl over his legs, he said, "Forty-five. And you?"

Finally, some truth from the man. "You already know, since day one."

"So, what do you want to know that my background check didn't uncover?" He ran a hand over Millie's dark curls.

"Why are you here?" It was the one thing nagging her this morning.

"Guarding Gardner."

And he lied.

"No, she's across the hallway. Why are you here in my apartment?" She pointed at the floor between them.

"Because you're here, and I need to keep you safe." He grabbed the hand that had pointed at the floor between them.

The truth.

"No, you need to keep her safe. That's your job. Nobody is paying you for my safety," Aurora pointed out her hand in his, not pulling it back.

"Nobody needs to. I want you safe. That's all that matters." He squeezed hers at his words.

"This is completely nuts," she said in a huff. He was completely nuts. There was one job he needed to do, but instead, he was over here.

"Why were you in reform school?" he asked from out of left field. How had he known she had attended one and not a regular school? How had he gotten that information.

"What do you mean reform school?" she asked as innocently as she possibly could as she pulled her hand from his. That was something she didn't want to talk about. Not now, not ever.

"You graduated from reform school." He wasn't letting her bypass the question.

Her gaze skittered away. "So? A lot of people graduate from places like that."

"What did you do?"

"Nothing awful."

"What, Aurora?" he asked seriously.

"Supposedly, I was operating a meth lab." She made it sound as if everyone got caught doing that.

"You? Before the age of eighteen?" he questioned.

"Hey, I could have pulled it off. I mean, I'm smart enough to have done it. Just not when they arrested me for it." She collapsed against the back of the couch.

He chuckled at her. "How old were you when the fucking cops caught her?"

Scowling at him, she said, "No swearing in front of Millie. She doesn't like to hear it."

Looking over at the baby, who was playing with a doll and not paying attention to them talking, he asked, "*That* Millie? She can't even talk yet."

"She can too, just not around you. She's shy around strangers. And even if she can't talk, she can listen."

"You're not answering the question."

"Fourteen, I was fourteen," she spat at him. He should be proud he got that out of her. He didn't deserve it.

"A meth lab at fourteen? Whose was it?" he asked in surprise.

"My grandmother's. She had been running them for years. I just got caught too close to one."

Or in the house, it was apparently close enough. It had been so long ago she couldn't remember all the details. But when it all came down to it, she was in custody, and her grandma wasn't. So, they charged her. Made an example of her.

"What happened to your grandma? Prison?"

Shaking her head, she said, "She left town and died a few months later in Atlantic City, New Jersey."

"She didn't get caught?"

"No, just me. Spent four years in reform school for that one. Graduated from there. At least I got out then and didn't have to go to prison." It had been so close to her reality, but Polly at the school had stood up for her. She'd told the parole board Aurora wasn't the same kid the police arrested anymore. The woman had saved her in the end. Something her own family hadn't done.

"You're serious? She never got caught?" He sounded surprised, but he hadn't known her.

"Nope. Grandma was a sly fox, Declan. Always something up her sleeve. Grandma rarely got caught. She was a master of what she did. I wouldn't be surprised if she faked her own death. It would be just like her to do it." She rubbed her hands together. *Yep.* It would be just like her.

"And yet, you sound envious."

"Oh, a little. She taught me so much before I went to reform school. I've always thought that she was grooming me to take over as head of the family, but it was really only my mother, so what kind of crime family is that?" she admitted. For two hookers, they'd only managed to have one child each, and they had needed far more than the three of us.

"Where is your mom?"

"In the wind. She could be anywhere. Just not dead yet," she said as a knock on the door sounded. Checking the clock, she saw it was 11:30 a.m. So it was the girls were coming to watch Millie.

Letting them in, she gave instructions to them about the care of Millie and headed out, Declan following. No way was she letting his presence get in her way or get her down. She loved her job, even if it was at one of the clubs she didn't love as much.

After spending the afternoon in her booth at the Bottoms Up club, with Declan right across from her most of the time, Aurora was tired of his presence. All day long, her lady bits were aware he was near, *so* aware that he was near.

By four in the afternoon, she was calling it a day so she could maybe get away from him for a moment. But she needed to swing by Rising Passions since she hadn't actually worked very long the day before. So now she was at her regular booth, but he was by the door talking to the bouncer of the day. Which gave her lady bits a moment of peace.

Tiff swung by with her mail and handed it off to her. Flipping through the bills and junk mail, she, of course, had received another letter. It was most likely late anyway. Slipping it unopened into her bag, she decided she would deal with it later. Bills she could deal with. Those were easy.

After an hour, she decided she'd had enough of work for the day and headed home. Declan drove with her, and they sat in silence. Once there, they took the elevator to the top floor, still in silence.

The silence stopped when they entered the apartment with the two young women who, with the help of Millie, were making supper for everyone. It was a surreal experience. Nobody had ever made her a meal at her place. Win liked takeout more than cooking, and so did Aurora.

Excusing herself, since the meal was not ready, she took the baby and herself to her bedroom and shut the door. The nanny thing was almost a hundred percent out. Aurora needed her space. There were too many people in her apartment right now for her liking.

Setting the baby down to play with her blocks, Aurora changed into leggings and a gray sweater. Settling on the floor, she pulled the letter from her briefcase. Opening it without Millie seeing her, she read what was written.

As she'd expected, it was another threat, another downgrade on the money amount, and it was received on Saturday, a day after the money was supposed to be dropped off. This time, it didn't include Heaven but instead referred to her as Aurora.

Between receiving the last one and now, she had decided it was her absent mom, Debbie. Debbie had to have found her somehow. But she was not getting these notes in enough time to actually confront the woman. But could she be behind the tire slashing? *Yes.* And the shootings? *No.* Her mom knew that if the target was dead, there was no payout.

Slipping the note back into her bag, she pulled Millie into her arms, and the baby let her mom rock her. Sensing that Aurora needed to be comforted, she didn't even try to get away. At least her baby didn't have a shitty mom.

There was a knock on the door, and Gardi poked her head in. "Aurora, supper is ready."

"Thanks. Gardi." Aurora got up, taking Millie with her.

"She was good today," Gardi said as they left her bedroom. "Really good."

"She usually is. I have a great daughter." Aurora smiled at the little girl in her arms. She loved it when people said her baby was great.

Gardi's usual smile faltered a little before she asked, "Do you have any more children?"

"Nope, just this one," Aurora said as they walked into the main part of the apartment.

The girls had made a meatloaf with potatoes, and it was great, better than takeout. Even Millie loved it. But once they were done eating and cleaning the kitchen, Aurora wanted to kick them out. She was done with them for today. Declan had headed to his place because he needed to get his stuff to stay with her for the week, so the girls stayed with her. Not that she needed protection, but Gardi needed it. So, she was going to protect the girl.

Looking over at the poor little rich girl who was slumming it in her club, Aurora couldn't help but see she was a natural with Millie. In fact, Reese was playing on her phone, and Gardi was on the floor talking to the baby. More than talking, she was adamantly talking with her hands and saying things over and over. But that was maybe a teacher thing since her degree was in teaching.

Over the past month, Aurora had noticed things about the girl. She didn't do well in groups, at least in large groups. Probably something about being raised as an actual princess. She liked to make eye contact when you spoke to her, every time, but sometimes didn't listen to you when you were not looking at her, especially in the club. As far as Aurora could tell, she would never be a stripper, not just because she had no tits, but because she couldn't dance—at all. Pole dancing class was a complete failure for her.

Today, her brown hair was hanging thickly down her back, and it was almost always in her eyes when she looked down. Rarely did she tuck it behind her ears so she could see. Glancing over at Reese, who had her hair in a ponytail, Aurora realized that she had never seen

Gardi do that with hers. Aurora wondered if it was a rich kid thing. Probably.

Since she was on her computer, she decided to do a search for Debbie Carlyle. See if she could find the woman and confront her about what she might be doing. And what had inspired her search in the first place.

"Aurora?" Gardi said from the floor.

"What?" She was looking through some sites.

"Have you ever had Millie's ears checked?" The girl ran her fingers over the outsides of them, making Millie giggle.

"Yes, they are fine." Aurora peeked up at her. What was she asking? Her kid could hear. She heard everything. Sometimes too much.

"It's just she doesn't talk much." Gardi was now looking at Aurora as if she knew the reason the baby didn't talk.

"She isn't ready. The pediatrician isn't concerned," Aurora said. Then she worried because the teacher was concerned, but Gardi was only a recent graduate. She couldn't know more than her pediatrician.

"Okay, but maybe when you take her in next you can ask," Gardi said, still looking at Aurora.

"Yeah, I will. Thanks." Aurora dismissed her and went back to researching Debbie.

Gardi let it go and went back to playing with the baby, who was loving all the attention. Millie loved anyone who would play with her one-on-one. Well, Millie loved everyone, even all the liars that were in her house right now.

A text came in on Aurora's phone, shifting her attention from her mom and those in the room to Win, who had abandoned her. It was a picture of a spoon that had an R in fancy scroll on the end of it.

Nice spoon. For someone important to you? Aurora

Just for you. Thought you would like it in your collection. Win

Just what I was looking for. Aurora

I had Daniel take it. Because he loves me. Win

You have corrupted him. Aurora

He was on the edge already. How are things there? Win

Okay. I don't want nannies. Aurora

Can't get rid of them. Are you at least having company at your place? Win

You're pretty sneaky. Letting those liars in your place. Aurora

I am. Win

Miss you still. Aurora

Dad and I talked a little, he admitted he gave up on me. Win

Sorry. I never gave up on you. Aurora

I never gave up on you either. Win

Are you getting yourself knocked up at his place? Aurora

Fuck no. Win

Good. Aurora

Have to go. Just making sure you're ok. Win

Putting down her phone, she smiled. All her worries were diminished when she talked to Win, even if they never talked about what was actually worrying her. Somehow, they had found each other at the moment each needed the other the most. And had each learned how to calm the other without even realizing they were doing it.

Win being with her family made Aurora nervous, not because she would ever lose her friend. But that it would send Win into a depression, and Aurora wouldn't be around for it. Daniel was the love of Win's life, but sometimes she needed Aurora. Over the years, Aurora had managed to keep it together—more than Win at times. But if Debbie was lurking around the edges of her life, what was she going to do?

CHAPTER
Twenty~Five

ALL WEEK, Aurora had changed her schedule. She left home at ten in the morning and went to her other clubs for a few hours, and then she went to Rising Passions for a few hours each day. Declan followed her everywhere. Spending his time watching to see if anything unusual happened and making sure she didn't do anything stupid.

And every night, Declan made sure he slept right beside her, something she was not complaining about. Everything else she was not impressed about. She spent most of their time together complaining about everything he was doing and about the fact that he lied to her. That she didn't let go of.

Mornings and evenings were spent with Millie. She loved her time with her daughter. She usually kicked the girls out after supper, which they always made, and spent the evening working and playing with her daughter. Once the baby was asleep, she spent another few hours working on her laptop and doing stuff for her clubs.

By Thursday, Declan was used to her new routine. By the time they had made it to Rising Passions, he could tell she was more on edge than she had been at Bottom's Up. It was the first time he had noticed that she was on edge all week. Usually, she was more relaxed at Rising Passions than at the other clubs, but not today.

"What's up?" he asked as she pulled into the parking lot.

"Nothing," she lied right to him.

"Aurora Carlyle, you're lying to me. What is wrong?" He called her out.

"I said nothing," she repeated, getting out of her SUV. She always drove.

Her eyes darted around the parking lot, trying not to let him see she was looking around today. Hurrying into the club, she must not have seen anything, but she had felt something. He was sure of it. Her sixth sense was sharper than his.

Once inside, she went to her booth and seemed to relax immediately. As her computer came out and her paperwork was in front of her, he went back out to the parking lot to see if anything was amiss. Wandering around, he checked out the spot that Paul King had been hiding in less than a week before. The connection to the dead man was still unknown to Declan. Aurora swore she had never heard or seen him, and he hadn't talked to Gardner yet, but it might just be time to lay it on the table with her too.

He hadn't wanted to get her involved in the situation, because she didn't know that he was hired to keep her safe. Now that he knew her better he knew she liked her freedom and he regretted that he was infringing on it. But he also knew he wanted her as safe as her dad did.

Now he wondered if he spoke to Gardner, that maybe some things would fall into place, and if she knew that she was in danger or causing others danger, she might just go back to her boring old life. Sure, Declan would be out of a job, but she at least might be safe. And he could concentrate on keeping Aurora safe.

After spending an hour outside looking around and not finding anything that looked or felt suspicious, he headed back into the club. Aurora was chatting with a couple of the employees, and since it looked like business, he headed back into the back of the club to look at the surveillance footage. So far, the only incident that was caught on tape was the Paul King shooting. Everything else was oddly out of reach of the cameras. Which smacked of an inside job.

King hadn't been looking for them. The other shooter had. The first night that he and Aurora had been shot at couldn't have been Paul King.

So, there were two shooters, but were they aiming at the same person? Could it actually be possible that King was after Gardner and someone else was after Aurora at the same time? It was crazy, but it explained a lot.

It'd been almost a week since the last incident, but that didn't mean anything around here. If the person was waiting for Gardner, then they were out of luck this week, and since Aurora had fired her, she shouldn't come back to the club again. If they were waiting for Aurora, she had been here every day this week, and nothing had happened.

Leaving the security room, he waited for her by the door. But she was not in her booth. Her briefcase was gone, and so was she. Running out the door, he saw that her SUV was still there. Walking around it, he noticed her briefcase in the backseat. But where was she? Looking around the lot, he went back inside, but the bouncer said she had left fifteen minutes before.

Back out in the sunshine, he walked around the SUV and saw no signs of struggling or a possible kidnapping. Pulling out his phone, he texted her.

DECLAN: Where are you?

AURORA: Relax, I'm fine.

DECLAN: WHERE ARE YOU?

AURORA: I'll come back for you in a bit.

DECLAN: WHERE THE FUCK ARE YOU?

Nothing came in after that. Kicking the tire of her SUV, he cursed. The moment he turned his back on her, she was in the wind. But how? Her SUV was right here. Was she walking?

No answers came to his questions.

All he had to do was wait for her to come back. She would at some point because this was her place. Not just her business but where she felt most at home. She would be back.

But until then, he was stuck there, worrying. At least Gardner was safe, but that was little conciliation with Aurora now in the wind.

CHAPTER
Twenty~Six

THE PARK WAS busy at four-thirty on a Thursday, and Aurora felt out of place in her heels and skirt. But this is where the drop-off was every week, and she needed to see it for herself. Whoever was sending her the notes had been here. They had been here today at noon, not that her mail had even been delivered by noon. Sitting on the bench that was always mentioned, so she looked around in case there was a clue.

It was a park with swings, slides, and open grassland. It reminded her that she should start bringing Millie to a park. Not this park; this park needed some help. Oddly, it was not far from where she had been raised, but she had never been here. Parks were not a part of her childhood.

More convinced than ever that it was Debbie who was sending her the letters, she still didn't know why. This would work better if she just walked up to her and demanded the money. Not that Aurora was ever giving that woman anything, but this dropping money thing was not working at all.

Next week, Win and Daniel were back, and they could watch Millie for a week so she could straighten this all out without having to worry about her daughter. By then, she would have shaken this odd group of cops, and she could camp out here all week, waiting on the woman. The blackmailer would show. She was still sitting at 25k in her demand. That was a lot of money for a Carlyle. They were small-bills people.

Looking around again, she tried to come up with where she was going to wait for the woman for hours. She decided to rent a car and surveil the place, but then she changed her mind. Debbie was doing that. Which meant Aurora would rent a dog and walk the park all day, looking in cars. That bitch was not getting away with this shit anymore.

Once the letters were figured out, then she could solve the shootings, which may have all been King. But it felt off. Could there actually be three cons going on at the same time?

Getting up, she walked back to Win's car. It still smelled, and she still had to get rid of it, but it always came in handy. Aurora was getting attached to the old beast. The smelly, smelly beast.

Back in the parking lot of the club, Declan was sitting on the hood of her SUV, pissed off. It had been over an hour, and she hadn't texted him back where she was. Parking the brown beast back where she had found it, she walked over to him.

"So, you are fucking alive?" he yelled at her.

"Yup, I'm not the one in danger!" she yelled back as she opened the SUV door and got in.

"How the fuck do you know?" he continued to yell at her but got into the passenger seat.

"Here I stand, and nobody is shooting at me," she pointed out.

This time, he tried not to yell. "You have to tell me when you leave."

"I have a fucking life, Declan. Sometimes, I just need to not have you stuck to me twenty-four-seven," she stated, peeling out of the parking lot.

"Some of those damn hours you enjoy."

"Some I do not."

He ran his hand up her leg. "Maybe I could make those more enjoyable."

She flicked his hand off her leg. "Fuck off, Declan."

Holding up his hands in defeat, he said, "I think I have to talk to Gardner about Paul King. I cannot get a handle on it."

"Maybe they were having an affair, and she threatened to tell his wife," Aurora said.

"Have you even met her? No way is she having an affair. She's probably saving herself for marriage," Declan pointed out.

"Maybe she's hiding that side of herself," Aurora suggested, though she was convinced the kid was as innocent as she presented herself.

"There is no *that side*, Aurora," Declan stated.

"I need to be there. You suck at your job." Aurora knew that he was a cop and looked at it from the angle of a cop. She was a criminal and looked at it like a criminal.

"I don't suck at this," he argued.

"You suck a little at this," she stated as she pulled into her garage.

As she drove to her spot, she slammed on her brakes. Both she and Declan jerked forward at her sudden stop. "Win is back."

"Is that the reason you tried to kill us?" Declan demanded.

Pulling into her spot, she ignored him, grabbed her briefcase, and headed to the elevator. She knew he was following and maybe still angry about the job critique, but sometimes it was true.

Pushing the button of the elevator, she stopped and waited. "You need to hire someone like me."

"A club owner?" he asked as the elevator doors opened for them, he had no idea how she could help him in his business.

"No, a criminal mind." She pushed the twenty-five button. "Someone who doesn't think like a cop."

He shook his head at her. "Cops tend not to recruit in prison."

"I have never been back to prison. Stupid criminals go to prison," Aurora said.

"So, you're smart enough not to go to prison again?"

"I don't do criminal things anymore. I'm a business owner, Declan, one with the skills you need." Aurora punched him in the shoulder, he was an ass sometimes.

On the top floor, they got out and headed down the hallway. "Don't talk to Gardi until I'm there."

"Wouldn't dream of it, Aurora," he said grudgingly.

Opening the door to her apartment, she was happy to see Win and Daniel were with the girls and Millie. The girls were making supper, and Win and Daniel were playing with the baby. Dropping her bag by the door, she breathed easy as Win got up and hugged her.

"Missed you," they said at the same time.

Win pulled out of her arms and held up a little silver spoon with a fancy R on it. "Spoon."

Aurora took the little spoon and hugged her again. "You stole from them."

"Daniel did. And they owe me," Win said.

"Daniel, I'm stealing your wife." Aurora didn't wait for an answer as she pulled Win into the bedroom.

Shutting the door, she sighed with relief. It had been a long week, and it wasn't even over. Having Win back would make it bearable—if only just a little. Now she would have all these people living with her.

"We came back early. A week was too long," Win admitted as she sat down on the bed.

"A week was too long. Was it terrible?"

"No, it was okay. Well, until this morning when my dad claimed that I made something of myself because of him. We had words, and I might have taken Summer and Autumn back with me. Though happily, they have their own apartment," Win admitted sheepishly.

"You went all Winter on them?" Aurora loved it when her friend let out her anger. Though she was more prone to keep it inside.

"I did. And I was maybe told I swear a lot." Win laughed.

Aurora smiled at her. "Good fucking thing you didn't take me."

"It was for the best." Win eyed her with suspicion. "Something is up with you."

"What?" she asked innocently, maybe too innocently.

"Your texts were off all week. You're hiding something from me. And not that you're getting fucked a lot, either. It's more. Though he's pretty hot, and so your type," Win said, looking over at the door to the apartment.

"He's a fucking cop," Aurora pointed out.

"Mostly just fucking, I think." Win laughed at her.

"Shut up. The darker-haired one is his kid. Seriously. His kid," she admitted, though now that she knew she couldn't *not* see the similarities, they even had a similar laugh.

Win shrugged. "Well, at least you don't have to raise her."

"The other one is a fucking princess," Aurora said.

"As in crown and all?" Win asked in surprise.

"No, just big big money. Someone is trying to kill her. Or me. We haven't decided yet."

Win sat up straighter. "Kill you? Why wasn't I told?"

"Nobody is trying to kill me. Declan just thinks so, but they are definitely after the kid." Aurora changed out of her skirt to leggings, not caring that Win was there. They had changed in front of each other so many times they didn't even think about it.

"I don't like that anyone thinks you're in danger," Win said.

"Declan has been with me twenty-four-seven since you left. I'm so tired of him."

"All twenty-four?" Win asked.

"Fuck you, Winter," Aurora stated.

"No, I think you're getting fucked enough. By Declan." Win said his name carefully.

"You're a bitch, Winter."

"That's what everyone says about me, still," Win said. She loved/hated her reputation at work. It hadn't changed much when she started to see Daniel.

"Did you get fucked in your teenage bedroom on your virgin bed?" Aurora asked.

"Yes, and on the desk and on the dresser and the rug will never be the same again," Win said, and Aurora laughed. "And one night we might have done it in the barn, might not have been at night."

And Winter was back in her life, with stories to tell of her adventures. Aurora was happy she had gone but was happier she was back. But now she had more people in her apartment. Opening the bedroom door, it was like she was having a fucking party, people everywhere. But the chicken was ready, so it was time to find a place to eat. Her table sat four and had never had this many people vying for a place to eat. She was as nervous as the table was about it.

CHAPTER
Twenty-Seven

DECLAN HAD MANAGED to snag a coveted spot at the table, along with Daniel and Win. The girls insisted Aurora get the last chair, the one by the high chair. Millie seemed maybe a little overwhelmed by so many people in one place. She was having a hard time deciding who was her favorite until she saw her mom. That was her favorite.

Aurora chatted with Millie as she fed her something orange from a jar. The day had seemed hard for the little girl, who was already in her pajamas and would have to be changed again after this meal since she was spitting out almost as much as she ate.

"So, how did the apartment work out, girls?" Daniel asked the two eating on the couch.

"Good," Reese answered.

"I'm sorry to say you're being evicted today. I need it back," Daniel said.

"With you guys home, I can send the girls home anyway." Aurora realized at that moment. With Win back, she didn't need sitters day and night. Or she did, but she didn't want them living with her or anywhere near her.

"I didn't realize." Gardi sounded disappointed at the fun being over early.

"Sorry, Gardi," Daniel said.

"Not your fault, Daniel," Gardi mumbled, but it actually was. Since they came back early, it was definitely their fault.

Silence fell in the room as everyone thought about the end of the week. Declan would have to tell Nick to follow Reese home, get Gardner settled, and have Rex there ready to take over. From now on, Reese would also have protection, at least for a while.

"Gardi, do you know who Paul King is?" Declan threw it out, and Gardner almost choked on her supper.

Coughing and sputtering, she said, "I used to work in his office uptown."

Declan had been sure that she would deny it. So, he pushed, "Directly with him? Or just near him?"

"Just near him. I only talked to him once," she admitted.

"About what?"

"A case he was working on with my boss."

"What kind of case?" Declan prodded.

"I can't say, it's confidential." She got to her feet but seemed unable to move beyond that.

"He tried to kill you on Friday. What was the case about?" He couldn't hold back. He needed more information.

Her face went pale, and she whispered, "A merger of two companies. Nothing that seemed important. It was just he didn't like me." Then she sat down but missed the couch and landed on the floor. Hard.

Win was out of her chair in a heartbeat rushing toward the girl. Helping her up, she led her back to the table and had her sit in Win's chair next to Aurora, who was watching her closely. Was she learning anything from being that close?

"Do you know if the case is still open, or is it already done?" Aurora asked.

"It's closed, has been since the day I talked to him. He's dead, isn't he?" Gardner's face was still pale, and she had her eyes closed.

Aurora was surprised Gardner hadn't heard anything about the man's death, there had only been a small write up about it in the newspaper. Young people didn't pay attention to anything that wasn't on their phones. A small time lawyer killed by senseless violence wouldn't rate all that high. And with everything happening around them, she wouldn't expected her to even look for information on him.

Not mincing words, Declan told her what she already knew, "Yes. Why would he try to kill you?"

She hugged herself. "I don't know."

"Do you want to tell just me?" Aurora took her hand in hers. "Why would he want to hurt you, Gardi?"

"I don't know," she said again.

"Who was he, Gardi?" Aurora pushed quietly.

"It doesn't matter anymore," Gardi said, barely above a whisper.

"Who was he, Gardi?" Aurora asked again in the same calm tone.

"My biological father," she whispered. Declan didn't even think anyone else heard her; she said it so quietly.

But he'd heard. What the fuck? Was she adopted, or did her mom have an affair? Or something else altogether. All he knew was that it didn't matter. She was still Royal Westmoreland's daughter, according to Royal Westmoreland.

"Did he know?" Aurora asked.

Declan didn't want to jump in since Aurora was getting the information they all needed. Her friendly tone had lulled the girl into talking. They should have talked to Gardi on Friday. She had all the answers after all.

"I didn't tell him, so I don't think so. He wasn't like I thought that he would be. I didn't like him, so I wasn't going to tell him. And then I got fired from the office, so I didn't think it would matter. Do you think he found out somehow?" Gardi asked Aurora.

She took Gardi's other hand in hers. "I don't know. How did you find out he was your father?"

"I took one of those genealogy tests. They matched me with people I'm related to. He was on the list. Maybe they contacted him. But why would he try to hurt me?" Gardner answered, and so much made sense for Declan, why so many dots didn't connect.

"I haven't figured that out yet. Why were you at the club?" Aurora had taken over the questioning.

"My birth mom works there," Gardner admitted.

"Do you think the place that did the test contacted him about you? But why kill you?" Win asked from behind Gardner, her hands on the girl's shoulders.

"I don't know if they would contact him, but maybe. Say they did, but why would he try and kill her?" Aurora asked.

From what she said, her life was no longer in danger since Paul King was dead. It was easy to see he had found out, but would that information be enough to send him over the edge? Especially since he'd made it his whole life without trying to kill someone else.

"Who is your birth mom?" Aurora asked because she knew her employees.

"It doesn't matter anymore. I don't want to meet her anymore," Gardner stated, pulling her hand away from Aurora's.

"Did you want to stay with Daniel and me for a few days? You can stay in Xander's room. He comes home on Sunday, and then we have a sofa you can crash on." Win asked before Declan could offer his own place. Though not as secure as Win and Daniel's, it would be close with him and Reese guarding the place.

"No, I want to go home." Gardner was looking at Aurora still.

Declan held out his keys to his daughter. "Reese, you can take my truck. I'll figure my own way home."

"Okay. We'll get our stuff." Grabbing the keys, Reese turned and left the apartment. Gardner silently followed.

Once the door closed, Win sat down in the chair again. "Holy shit."

"No fuck," Aurora agreed, not caring that Millie was there to hear her swear.

"Who do you think the mom is?" Win sat back down in her chair.

"I don't know." Aurora got up and tossed the little jar of baby food in the garbage.

"How many women over forty do you even employ? This woman would have to be over forty, right?" Declan asked, starting to clean the kitchen.

Moving was his way of working through difficult situations. So loading the dishwasher and putting the leftovers in the fridge made his mind work better. Not that anyone else seemed to notice, they seemed to want to talk over the situation.

Aurora was silent for a moment before saying, "Four total, I think."

"Do you think she's lying?" Win asked, all eyes turned to her. "I mean about the mom thing. Strippers aren't usually over forty. Do you think she's looking for a sibling instead?"

Declan couldn't see her lying about looking for a parent instead of a sibling. A sibling would be so much easier than a parent. "That could be anyone."

"How old is Gardner?" Win asked.

"Twenty-three." Declan was seeing why Win would think sister, a younger woman would make more sense.

"What are you thinking, Winter?" Aurora asked, crossing her arms. The two could tell when the other was on to something. Had for a long time.

"Green eyes, she'd have been born around the time you were arrested," Win said.

Aurora just glared at her. "Nope. One hundred percent no. Debbie had a botched abortion when I was seven, no more kids."

"Are you sure?"

"Oh yeah. That was a day to celebrate, more than any of my birthdays. You don't forget that. But Grandma had two kids I never knew about. I have very little information on either one of them, but maybe through them. A cousin? I'm stretching really thin on this." Aurora was spitballing.

This was more information than she had voluntarily given since Declan had met her. Just a fountain of information. It seemed that Win had no clue about most of it either, based on the surprised expression on her face. It seemed some secrets were so deep even her best friend didn't know about them.

Win asked. "I leave for a few days, and you suddenly have more relatives than I have ever heard about? Did you actually look for your mother while I was gone?"

"Yes, she isn't dead. Or in prison. Much to my regret," Aurora admitted to her friend.

"So, no file in the cake?" Win asked.

"No family fucking reunion." Aurora laughed, and Win joined in, relaxing them both.

A knock on the door made them both stop laughing immediately. Reese was at the door. Aurora jumped up, grabbed Millie, and thanked both girls for taking the time to watch Millie for her during the week.

As the girls left, Gardner reminded Aurora to have the baby's ears checked as soon as she could. Aurora absent-mindedly agreed she would do it and waved them off. Back inside, he looked at her questioning.

"Gardi thinks that there is something wrong with Millie's hearing. I'll have it looked at just because she got me nervous about it," Aurora admitted, kissing the baby's head.

Win took the baby from Aurora. "I've never noticed anything."

Daniel looked at the ears in question. "Me neither."

Declan excused himself to Aurora's bedroom to call his team to get them in position for Gardner's return home and for someone to be on Reese for a few days. When that was done, he went back out to the main part of the apartment and saw Aurora was alone, washing the rest of the dishes at the sink.

Walking up behind her, he slid his arms around her. "Missing your girls now?"

"Yes, they should have stayed to do the dishes," Aurora said, leaning into him.

"Has the criminal mind connected the dots yet?" He kissed her neck.

"Working on it. Do you have cops on Gardi? And on Reese?"

"Yes, dear. I have *security* looking out for them. Nick is on Gardner, and Rex will be there when Reese gets home." He couldn't stop kissing her bare skin. The hours since he had kissed her had been too long.

"Did you know that Westmoreland wasn't Gardi's dad?" She stopped doing the dishes completely and leaned into the kisses.

"No idea. I'll have to talk to him. Maybe he knows who the mom is. He really didn't care that she was working at the club. Like he half expected it or something."

Aurora pushed him away to turn to him. "Really? He was all okay with her working at the club?"

Slipping his hands under the sweater, he slid them around to her back. "Yes. Maybe Win was onto something. That you and Gardner share a father."

"That one we will never know. Hooker's kids don't have fathers. And I have never had a DNA test to see who it might be. I think the road ends there," Aurora told him.

"Okay, not you. Can we look over your books?" he asked tentatively, sure she wouldn't let that ever happen.

"I don't think it matters. She's back home, not working at the club, and so will have no contact with the woman," Aurora stated the obvious.

"I beg to disagree, but I know you need to sit with the idea for a while. So I'll play with Millie so you can think it over." Teasing them he kissed her neck again and let her go.

Over the week, she had relaxed with Millie and him. No longer did she guard her like a mama bear when he was around. Sitting down near his daughter, he knew exactly how pissed Aurora was going to react when he told her he was her father. But he was going to have to. Because he was never going to *not* be there for his kids.

Millie toddled over to him and gave him a red block. Then she toddled away to get another one. Millie could do this all day. In fact, he had spent many an hour doing it. When the baby's back was to him, he said her name. Quietly and then louder when she didn't turn to look at him. He clapped his hands as loud as he could. Still no reaction. She picked up a yellow block, which she brought happily to him.

Turning to see if Aurora had noticed, he saw she was standing on the other side of the couch, just watching them. Her voice quivered as she admitted, "She can't hear."

"Tomorrow, we will get her in tomorrow," Declan stated. "I'm sure she's just not paying attention."

"Gardi was right," Aurora whispered, watching her baby pick up blocks one at a time.

That night, Millie slept soundly between him and Aurora, both watching her closely. Neither seemed able to sleep themselves.

"She's okay, you know. Gardi's just putting ideas in our heads. She doesn't know anything." Declan assured her, as they watched the baby sleep soundly between them.

Aurora wanted to touch her daughter, but didn't want to wake her up so just adjusted the blanket around her, "I've known Millie her entire life, if there was an issue I would have known about it already."

"You're an amazing mom, no way you would have missed something like that." He took her hand and held it.

The room slipped into silence, during their conversation neither had whispered. Neither believed what they were saying, nothing was wrong with the baby. But tomorrow would be soon enough to face that fact.

AURORA DIDN'T MAKE it to any of her clubs that Friday. The entire day was spent in the hospital with Millie, test after test was performed on her. There was little talk about passing or failing them, just another round of them. Declan was with her the entire time. She hadn't asked him to accompany her, but she was glad he was there.

In the middle of the night, she decided that she wouldn't tell Win until she actually knew anything. She didn't have to know that Aurora was being overly cautious with Millie.

"Millicent Carlyle." A nurse called her baby's name. Would Millie ever hear her name in a waiting room?

Once in the office, the doctor came in. He was not a happy doctor who thought that Millie was adorable and hitting all of her milestones. He was grouchy and barely looked at the baby. She had been examined earlier in the day by another doctor.

"I'm sorry to say she's almost completely deaf at this point. I think she was able to hear at birth but has lost the ability since then, which points to congenital hearing loss. From the tests we have done, it looks like it is inherited. We would like to test both of you to see which one of you carries the gene."

His words destroyed Aurora's world.

Tuning out the doctor, she looked at Millie's smiling face. Was it because she swore too much? Couldn't her tiny ears handle it? It had to be her fault. She was her mom. A mom who had been everything to the baby since the beginning.

The doctor piled them with pamphlets about things from deafness to what can be done about it. Trying not to cry, she took the papers, and Declan took Millie from her. He gently pushed her out the door. She was numb and took the blood test that they requested. Declan took the test also, right beside her. She was unable to question him in her current state.

Driving back to her apartment, she knew she shouldn't, but she couldn't be a passenger either. She couldn't have a panic attack today. Today was for complete numbness.

When they make it home safely she locked herself in the bedroom, letting Declan take care of Millie, who couldn't hear her mom. Lying in bed, she knew that she was being punished for her misspent youth through her daughter. This was her fault—all of it.

Deciding to drown herself in work, she pulled out her computer and started working on the books for the month. It was soon time to go over them with Win, and she hadn't even looked at them. So many nights of no profit from when the cops were called was going to be noticeable.

Flipping through the employees, she wrote down the names of Gardi's possible mother. Tiff at the bar; she had been there forever and had two adult kids. But if Tiff was her mother, she would have kept her. Aurora left her a possible. Laurie, who came in during the early morning hours to clean, was old enough, barely. But Laurie was also Hispanic, or at least part Hispanic. No way was she the princess's mom. Jill was her other possibility, but she would have been nine when Gardi was born, so she was out. So, only Tiff was a possibility.

On the background website, she looked up Tiff and was surprised the woman actually had no record, none. Maybe she wasn't who she had always said she was. She had been with Aurora since before she had owned the club. Tiff had started as a stripper and moved to bartending when she got tired of stripping. Aurora couldn't remember her there when she was in college, but she must have been. She would have to ask Win if she remembered her from back then.

Then she typed in the names that had been on the edge of her mind since yesterday. Donnie Carlyle, the uncle she had never heard of. But if he was a Carlyle, he had a record of some sort. Sure enough, he'd stolen a car at nineteen and smashed it into a tree. The tree had, of course, won. It was around the time she was ten, which meant she should have remembered him being around since he should have been home. Sylvia had, after all, lived with Debbie and her most of the time.

Digging deeper, she caught a break and found an article with a picture of Donnie Carlyle in it. The article was about a school that was training kids to be contributing members of society. It was a school for the deaf. Donnie had been deaf, like her Millie.

The picture was just the proof she needed. It was her. She had the bad genes and had given them to Millie. Did Millie have the addiction gene? The hooker gene? What else had Aurora unloaded on her baby girl?

Back to the computer, she tried to find Dawn Carlyle but couldn't find any information on her. Was she deaf too? Did her grandma give them up when they were deaf? *Of course, she did.* Her grandmother was a heartless bitch. No way was she keeping kids that would be a burden to her. But maybe Dawn got out and was adopted by someone who loved her and treated her like she deserved.

Looking back on the website she had paid to use, she looked at Dawn's birthdate, which was too old for Gardi. She was five years older than Aurora. But possibly Gardi was Dawn's daughter. It could fit. Could Dawn be Tiff? Tiff certainly hadn't been treated like she deserved by her loved ones—not if she'd spent her working life in a strip club. And why would Tiff never say anything about it? And Tiff was not deaf. If Dawn was not deaf, then Grandma would have kept her. It was a circle.

Then again, if Dawn was Gardi's mother, Gardi might think Aurora could find her. Aurora grunted. *Not hardly.*

Tossing the computer away from her, she flopped down on the bed, fully dressed and fully depressed. She texted Win that she needed her now.

Within minutes, Win came into the bedroom carrying Millie. "Declan said he thought you needed her now. He went to see Daniel. If your life is being threatened, he's over there."

"Thanks." Aurora didn't get up from her spot, looking at her white ceiling.

"What's up?" Win closed the computer and put it on the nightstand.

"I have completely destroyed my daughter's life," Aurora admitted as her daughter lay down on her stomach with a smile.

Win sat down cross-legged on the bed. "She looks like she's okay, Aurora."

"She can't hear," Aurora admitted, hugging her baby to her.

"That's just some kid saying it, Rora. Millie's fine."

Aurora shook her head and forced the tears back. "We took her in for tests today. The doctors say she can't hear. We have a consultation in a week about what to do."

Win's eyes widened, then narrowed. "It's not your fault Aurora. You didn't make her deaf." Win patted the baby on the back as she still lay on her mother's stomach.

"It's inherited," Aurora said in a whisper.

"So, she has a dad." Win pointed at the dark hair and gray eyes. "But it doesn't matter anyway. Assigning blame doesn't change anything. We should be focusing on what's best for Millie instead."

"It's me. I found that my grandmother gave up two kids; one was deaf, and the other is lost. It's me. They ran a test today, and it will say it's me," Aurora said.

Win clasped her hand and grew earnest. "'I know this isn't what you imagined for Millie, and it will be challenging, but you're a great mom, and you will continue to be a great mom. This baby is lucky to have you."

"But I promised her that her life would be perfect," Aurora argued.

"Her world still will be, just a different perfect. A better perfect." Win winked. "And since she will have a disability, I bet she will be a shoo-in for Rosewood Academy."

"Fuck Rosewood Academy," Aurora said with a laugh. Realizing that she didn't have to stop swearing, Millie couldn't hear it anyway.

"What does Declan say?"

"Not much, but he went with me. I didn't even ask him to." Aurora sat up, feeling better with Win there.

Win nodded and took Millie into her arms, "She's his, isn't she?"

"Yup. He's changed a bit since back then, but it's him. I wasted so much time looking for him for he to just walk into my strip club. " Aurora said, got out of bed, and started pacing the room.

Though she hadn't been fully away in the parking lot, he had changed quite a bit. But when he sat across from her in the club she had recognized him. And seeing him and Millie together had cemented everything. Except how she was going to tell him about his baby.

"Only you could find the same guy twice in this city. Does he know?" Win watched her with Millie in her arms.

Aurora looked out the window and went back to the bed and Win. "Yeah, since he saw her. No way he couldn't tell."

"What are you going to do about it?"

"I don't know. At this point, there's still someone out there that he thinks is trying to kill me and or Gardner." She paced back to the window.

"I might be a little concerned about that also," Win pointed out.

"Don't be. They're after Gardi," Aurora assured her as she kept moving.

"I don't think you're taking this very seriously. So, I'm happy a cop is in your bed and following you around," Win said, tapping the bed she was on.

Aurora sat down. "He's nice to have in my bed. I could use a little less of him elsewhere."

"I don't want to hear about it," Win stated flatly.

"Yes, you do." Aurora laughed from her flat position.

"Only if you want to share, but I'll share also. We also snuck down to the kitchen one night." Win laughed about her trip to her father's.

"You're never going to be invited back." Aurora laughed with her.

"I don't want to go back. I'm okay with two sisters; the rest I don't need. Maybe two sisters will be too much also," Win admitted.

Aurora sat up a little. "Hey, do you remember Tiff working at the club when we were in college?"

"No, but didn't she come from like Chicago or something? Wasn't her stripper name something Chicago-related?" Win asked.

Flopping back, Aurora said, "She was the only one I could come up with. Everyone else is too young or too dark."

"Maybe the other club?" Win asked. "Didn't you find her at the other club?"

"I did, but why would she be all okay with working at the wrong club?"

"Because our club is the best club?" Win guessed.

Sitting up, Aurora grinned. "You got that right."

Win ran her fingers through Millie's dark hair. "A Bonus of her being deaf. You can be as loud as you want in here."

"Only you would think of that Winter." Falling back on the bed, Aurora looked at the ceiling again.

"Are you feeling better now so I can go home and have sex with my husband?" Win asked.

"Yes, don't let Declan join in. I don't want him to see how wild and crazy it can get. He's like a decade older than Daniel." Aurora hugged Millie to her again.

"I'm pretty sure you're pretty wild and crazy yourself."

"I might be, but I have never fucked in a strip club." Aurora watched Win flip her the bird as she left the room.

Nothing had changed, but Win had made her see it wasn't the end of the world. Maybe Declan could have told her that, but from Win, it was more believable. They had seen the end of the world together over the years. They knew how to bring themselves back from it.

Soon enough, Declan came into the room and took over care of Millie, well, just making sure she didn't roll off the bed.

Aurora was still back down on the bed, looking at the ceiling. "It comes from my side."

He picked up Millie from the bed. "How do you know?"

"Research, I'm pretty good at it. I had an uncle who was deaf. Possibly an aunt."

"But you didn't know that before?" Declan asked in confusion.

"I found information on the web that Grandma sent them away. They would have been useless to her," Aurora admitted the dirty truth of her family.

"Millie's amazing either way, not useless at all." Declan patted Millie's diapered butt.

"She's still my perfect baby." Aurora pulled her up and kissed her on her cheeks. Making her baby giggle.

"I think she can sleep in her own bed tonight," Declan announced.

"Me too." Aurora finally willingly agreed with one of his plans.

GARDNER WESTMORELAND HAD YET to leave her estate. It had now been a full week since she had dropped the paternity bomb. It had gone off in a pop and then nothing. His team had been watching her around the clock again, and so far, she hadn't ventured off the property. Nor had anyone ventured on to it.

But now Declan had a meeting today with Royal Westmoreland himself. Following a butler from the door to Westmoreland's office, he looked at the world that Gardner was raised in and didn't see her bubbly personality fitting into the sterile house. She fit better in a small place that would be full of her personality, not here with all the do-not-touch furniture.

In the office, the butler silently left as Royal stated, "Hello there, Mr. Chamberlain."

"Mr. Westmoreland."

"The staff says that Gardner is back at the house and hasn't been leaving anymore. It seems her wild oats have been sowed." Royal laughed at his daughter.

"I don't know if she's done with the wild oats, Mr. Westmoreland. I think she's scared to leave right now," he told the man.

Today, he had left Aurora for the first time since she had left him at the club the week before. Since then, he hadn't let her out of sight. Not that she had tried to sneak away again. He just hoped he had finally convinced her that her life was in danger.

Even if he wasn't there, Rex was watching her. From the parking lot, but still there. It was only for an hour or so while he took care of this meeting. And if he could have rescheduled it, he would have. But nobody reschedules Royal Westmoreland.

"Why would she be scared? Well, beyond being her usual Gardner self—scared of her own shadow sometimes."

Royal didn't seem to know his daughter well. If she was scared of her own shadow, she never would have ventured into any strip club, much less worked at one.

"Someone was murdered at the club last week," Declan said.

"The club?" Westmoreland questioned with concern.

"The strip club she was working at. She's been fired until things settle down."

"I hope that she wasn't in danger there, Mr. Chamberlain? I pay you good money to make sure she isn't in actual danger." There was an edge to his voice.

"We were able to protect her. Why was she working at a strip club, Sir?" Declan asked, point blank.

"I'm sure she's looking for her birth mother, but she won't find her. I have no idea where that woman could possibly be. Probably dead." Royal still seemed unconcerned about Gardner trying to find this woman.

"So, she was looking for her birth mother all along. That would have been good information to have when I took this job." Declan watched the man behind the desk show no emotion at all.

"I don't think about it much. My first wife wanted a baby, but she couldn't have children. I, um, came up with a way to make things right for all of us. I arranged for us to get a baby. Unfortunately, my first wife died when Gardner was seven. I remarried after, and we have two children together. Gardner is Gardner." The man actually shrugged at his daughter. It didn't sound like he was a doting father to his firstborn.

Leaning toward the man, Declan said, "The man who was killed at the club last week was her birth father. He was trying to kill her."

"The hell you say!" Royal yelled and threw the pen he was holding across the room, and it hit the wall. He finally showed emotion for his child. At least that got a reaction out of the man. Some emotion for his kid, even if she was adopted.

"It seemed she got her DNA tested and found her real father. But she didn't tell him that he was a father."

"Fuck that old fucking bitch. Of course, I see it now. That kid is nothing like me." Royal slammed his hands onto his desk. Declan wondered if he even heard what he was saying.

"Excuse me?"

"That old fucking woman who arranged for my first wife and I to get a baby swore that the kid was mine. I gave her enough fucking money for it. And now you're telling me I'm not even her fucking father?" Royal slammed his hands on his desk again.

Declan sat back, wondering what the fuck this man was even talking about. He was nuts, and not in a good way. He'd raised Gardi as his daughter. Surely, he had some feelings toward her beyond biological responsibility.

"Sir, about Gardner, I still feel she's in danger." Declan tried to get the conversation back to what was important: Gardner's safety.

"Mr. Chamberlain, I don't fucking care about her. What little concern I had is now gone. She isn't even my child. All this time, I have been a fool." His harsh words shocked Declan.

"She's still your's. You raised her," he reminded the older man.

"She'll not be left destitute," he spat out as if money would be enough for Gardner. Bubbly, fun Gardner.

"She needs more than money, sir." From what little time he had spent with her, he knew she was more than a spoiled rich kid. So much more.

That got the old man's attention, the word *money* in a conversation. "Are you having sex with my daughter, Mr. Chamberlain?"

"Good god, no. But I have spent the last few months getting to know her, and I think she's a great girl." Declan had no way to describe her.

"Great girl? No, she's a burden that I was never getting rid of, Mr.

Chamberlain. But now she's no longer my burden. I can wash my hands of her. Have you ever tried to find a willing husband for a kid who is retarded? Now I don't have too." Royal actually laughed at his own words. Was it a joke? Because what he was saying was not funny.

"Are you kicking her out then? Today?" Declan needed to know what to do with his team and with her. No way was he not going to keep protecting her as long as she needed it. Not that long ago, she had wanted to move in with Reese. That sounded a lot better right now than it did then. Reese had proved herself to be more than just protection for Gardner, but a friend.

"I'll have my lawyer come up with something. As for time, Faith would like to have had her gone years ago. I sent her to boarding school for years to get her out of our hair. Then college out of state."

"She spent last week living with my daughter, and they are friends. Could I just take her today? She can move in with her?" Declan lied.

Reese was back in the dorms, but she had a bedroom at his house Gardner could stay in. It was better than this place, but then almost anywhere was.

"Let me think for a moment." Royal dismissed him and waved him out of the office. The butler was there to close the door. Standing in the hallway, he looked at the pictures on the wall. They were all pictures of old men with serious expressions. Nothing really to look at.

As the time ticked by, the butler didn't leave his side. But Declan was left wondering about Gardner's awful relationship with her family. They didn't want her around, and it seemed they might not have spent a lot of time hiding it from her.

It seemed Royal had knocked up some woman who wanted a baby, and then that woman had died. Were they even together during that time? What had their relationship been?

The butler let him back into the office, and Royal Westmoreland was pleased as punch behind his desk. "She's all yours, Mr. Chamberlain."

In the chair he had been in earlier was Gardner, but not the Gardner he had known—a dejected Gardner. When she looked up and saw him, she didn't even register that they had spent days together with Aurora and Reese just the week before. Her face was completely blank of emotion.

"My lawyers were able to get everything organized in no time. Gardner has signed everything I need her to sign. You can take her." Royal dismissed them both, treating his own daughter like a dog he was giving to a new owner. A dog he had never liked or wanted.

This wasn't the first time Gardner had been dismissed because she got up and walked out of the office without a word, a look, or even a protest. What she had been forced to sign, Declan couldn't phantom. But now she was free of the man, not that Declan knew what he was going to do with her.

In the hallway, she turned in another direction, and the butler made sure he didn't follow her. The butler led him to the front door, saying, "She's being packed up right now. Her SUV is by the garage."

"Why is he doing this?"

"If she isn't a Westmoreland, she isn't a Westmoreland," was all the snooty butler said.

Getting into his truck, he drove over to the mentioned garage. It seemed he had just gotten another daughter. He had even less of an idea of what to do with this one.

Not knowing what to do, he called Aurora. Maybe she would have an idea. When she answered with her stern Aurora voice, he said, "I had a meeting with Westmoreland today. It went kind of south."

"You're so shitty at your job," was all she said, but he recognized the teasing tone in her voice.

"I'm not. But I told Westmoreland that Gardner had been shot at and by whom. Which might have been a huge mistake," he admitted.

"What? Is he going to force her to live in a bubble of bulletproof glass? Never to see the outdoors again?" Aurora's words made him smile at the woman. She tried to be so touchy all the time but was just all soft and gooey for anyone she cared about.

"No, that is what we would do. I think he disowned her. Her stuff is being packed even as we speak." Declan watched a box being put into the SUV by a man he had never seen before.

"You're not just letting her drive away to god knows where. This city will kill her," Aurora's voice was on edge.

"I told Westmoreland I would take her. I had to." Another box was added.

"You're such a softy. Have whoever you have watching the place drive her stuff here to the club. We can all meet up and have a meeting about this. Decide from here. Maybe she knows where she wants to be. She's an adult. And maybe her dad will change his mind one day," Aurora said.

"I don't think so. He actually called her an unmarriageable retard. I almost punched his lights out for that. She has a fucking college degree." Declan shook his head as another box was loaded in the SUV. Was everything going to fit in there?

"Fucking bastard. I have to go. Come to the club with her," Aurora stated.

"I will," he said as if the club was the center of the world or even safe. But to Aurora, it was. That much he had learned these last weeks. If any of this shit had happened at her other club, she would have taken it more seriously. But her club was her safe place. Even Win came to the club when they needed to feel safe and loved.

But the club was where everything had gone down since he met her. Every shooting and mischievous activity had happened at her club. Now, he was bringing Gardner back to it. And sadly, even to him, it felt right to bring her back there.

CHAPTER

Thirty

HANGING UP WITH DECLAN, Aurora reread the letter from today's mail. Today's letter was at least not late, but only because there was no drop-off time or location. The blackmailer was done with that now.

Getting up, she was shaking with anger. No way was that woman destroying her life. Because today she had threatened Millie. *Her Millie.* No way was that woman even ever going to think about her daughter.

Heaven, if you don't give me $100,000, I will kill your daughter. I'll meet you at your club, I know when you're there.

It wasn't signed, but Aurora knew exactly who it was. And no fucking way was she giving her any money. A quick call to Penny settled her nerves. Millie was taking a nap, and Penny had assured her that nobody unwanted got into their gated community. But she also said that once she woke up, she would bring the kids to Daniel at the apartment. It would be safer there on the top floor.

Setting down her phone, she sat and waited. For once, she didn't work. She didn't watch to make sure everyone was working. She just waited. Rex was here, but so was the gun she had started to carry last week. She hated guns and didn't want to, but Declan had insisted she be able to protect herself.

Her mother was as stupid as her Grandmother had always thought she was. It would have been easy for Aurora to have had the cops waiting for her arrival. If she had more than a few hours, she might have done just that, but instead, she was doing this alone.

As if materialized by magic, a gray-haired woman slid into the booth across from Aurora. She was nothing like Aurora thought she would be. Her hair was unkempt, and her eyes were wild, the same green as Aurora's, but completely wild, darting from here to there and back again. Whatever drugs the woman had taken over the years had never completely left her system.

"Heaven," she stated.

"Debbie," Aurora stated back in annoyance.

"Do you have my money?" Debbie Carlyle demanded.

"I don't have that kind of fucking money. This is a strip club, not a money machine." Aurora waved her hand around the room.

"You have more than one," Debbie stated, her eyes not focusing.

"I still don't have that kind of money, and I'm not giving you a fucking penny of what I do have." Aurora was unable to look away from those crazy eyes. They were still green, but nothing like her own anymore.

"You owe me." Debbie's voice faltered.

Aurora laughed loudly. "I owe you nothing. You let me rot in reform school."

"I tried to get you out. Well, I would have, but you ran a meth lab, they weren't letting you out. Mom took off. I haven't seen her since." Debbie tried but failed at her excuses.

"She's dead. Since a few weeks after I was picked up." Aurora didn't soften the news. Her mother didn't deserve it.

"No, my mom isn't dead. Nothing kills my mom," Debbie argued, even though she hadn't seen the woman for two decades.

"Cars kill your mom. Dead as a doornail, New Jersey," Aurora told what she knew, which was still very little.

"No wonder she never came back. She got some money from some-where and took off. I was sure she'd be back when she spent it. That's what always happened before." Debbie leaned back in the booth. Which would require a heavy cleaning after the woman finally left.

"Who were Donnie and Dawn?" Aurora wanted to hear it from someone who knew.

"Retards, mom kept Donnie a few years and then gave him up to the state. Dawn, she gave up for adoption when she was, say, two, dumb as a brick."

"You mean they were deaf?" Aurora needed to know.

"Curse of the Carlyle's. I was lucky you never got that. But of course, your kid did." Debbie smirked.

Glaring at her mother, Aurora wondered how she had even known that Millie was Deaf. She barely knew herself. It had only been confirmed a week before. Her mom was in no way that computer-savvy.

"I'm not giving you any money. But I am turning you in for stealing my identity," Aurora said. It was over; she had all the information she ever needed from this woman.

"Not a chance, you owe me. Big time. And you weren't using your identity anymore anyway," Debbie stated.

"I owe you nothing. Everything I have I did for myself." And Winter, she didn't add. It was because of Winter and her pushiness that Aurora was here today and not like her mother.

"I'm head of the family," Debbie stated proudly, showing her missing teeth in her smile.

"There's no family, Debbie. There is just you, and you're nothing. Grandma would be so disappointed in you." Aurora twisted the knife. Debbie wanted nothing but her mother's approval.

Debbie scowled. "Liar, she would be proud of me. I almost got twenty thousand out of that King idiot before he, uh, got shot."

"You mean when you shot him? Because that's what happened. But were you blackmailing him?" Aurora's mind was piecing together everything. Had it all been Debbie?

"Nobody said I was doing anything."

Aurora laughed at her mother, "You didn't get any money from him before he died, did you?"

"He had the money, so who knew he would just go after the girl?

She's pretty worthless. Not much Carlyle in that one." Debbie's eyes darted around again.

"Whose is she? Yours?" Aurora demanded. This was ridiculous.

Debbie's eyes actually both focused on Aurora, and she laughed, "Fuck Heaven, how many drugs have you taken in your life? That girl is your kid."

"Bull." Aurora breathed out the words.

"This is precious. You can't even remember." Debbie laughed again, her eyes back to darting around the room.

"Get out of here, Debbie, and if I see you again, I'll have you arrested," she warned her just once.

"I'll go when I want, *Heaven*," Debbie emphasized her name.

"Then I'll shoot you, and they will arrest you in the hospital. I have seen your rap sheet, Debbie, or should I say Heaven? Either way, you're screwed." Aurora pulled her gun and pointed it right at her mom.

"You don't have the balls. You never did," Debbie said.

"You know what, Debbie? I want you in prison. And I won't bring you a cake." Aurora said and winged her mother in the shoulder.

Her mom yelped in pain.

"What are you talking about?" Her mom's eyes went wide. Looking straight at her daughter, she grabbed her now wounded shoulder. "I was *leaving*."

"I changed my mind. I want you in prison," Aurora said again.

"An ambulance is on its way, Aurora," Tiff said as she walked by, calmly like this happened all the time around here.

"Heaven!" her mother hissed as blood ran through the fingers holding her wound. Sirens sounded outside. Aurora rolled her eyes. More cops at the strip club.

"I hope you enjoy prison. It really got me onto the straight and narrow," Aurora said as paramedics came into the building, along with six cops, all worth it even if it was Friday.

"I hate you," Debbie said again.

"Hello, officers." Aurora got up and met the cops. "There was a little accidental discharge of a gun. Her name is Debra Carlyle or Heaven Carlyle, and she has a few arrest warrants you might be interested in. And there was a man who was shot outside the club last week, and I'm pretty sure she's the trigger man."

"We'll look into it." The cop seemed to catch onto what she was saying.

It took less than ten minutes for the cops to leave this time; the ambulance had left within five. Per Officer Hartman, Debbie was going to be charged with the shooting of Paul King, the man she had been blackmailing.

Looking at the booth with her mom's blood on it, she was happy the bullet hadn't even damaged the seat back. Just a neat little hole was left. She could live with that. And now she had a souvenir of her mother's arrest.

An Angry Rex came out from the back room. "What the fuck happened out here?"

"Nothing for you to be concerned about, Rex. Oh, and there are cameras back there, so if you don't want me to show your boss, I wouldn't say anything about this," Aurora answered.

"Damn, someone locked me in the john." he said glared at her, and the waitress by the bar.

Aurora glanced her way and knew there would be a little extra in her next pay check for that move. She had asked her to distract him, and had given her permission to do whatever it took to distract him for at least an hour. She did even better then Aurora had expected her to do.

"Could I get this booth cleaned up? I'm leaving for the day as soon as Declan gets here," he announced and grabbed her briefcase.

Outside in the sunshine, she tossed her briefcase into the backseat next to Millie's car seat. Millie was safe, Gardner was safe, and so was Aurora. But now she had to find a place for Gardner to live, and she had to figure out what to do with Gardner, her daughter.

Did she remember having a baby? Sometimes. But she had been thirteen at the time, under the complete control of her grandmother. For most of the pregnancy, she hadn't even known she was pregnant because she was thirteen. The rest was spent not getting attached. Grandma had plans for the baby. Aurora didn't know the plans or even want to know them. This was just another job for her. It was the same as telling every man her grandma gave her to that she was a virgin. It was her job. Mom was no better, just a lower class of clients with her mom.

Sitting in her SUV, she wondered what she was going to say to the girl. Gardner knew she was her mom, and she had known the day she had walked topless across Aurora's strip club. She had known last week when she said she no longer wanted to meet her mom. To know her at all.

And now that she had been disowned by her father, she only had Aurora. Sure, Aurora loved Millie, but Millie was hers. Gardner had never been hers. She barely remembered carrying her, birthing her. She had so easily forgotten her.

The Carlyle curse, yes, she had heard of it. Her grandma would always say at least Aurora hadn't gotten the Carlyle curse. Now she knew what it was: deafness.

Thinking back on the conversation, she wondered if her mother even knew about Millie. Was all the daughter talk actually about Gardner the entire time? No, there was no way Gardner was deaf. Aurora had had conversations with the girl—many of them. She had worked as a waitress for weeks, a poor one, but there hadn't been that many complaints.

"Fuck, fuck, fuck," she said to her empty car. How the fuck did she have a twenty-three-year-old daughter? What the fuck did she do with a twenty-three-year-old daughter? She needed to talk to Winter right now.

But before she could dial the phone, a Lexus SUV pulled into the parking lot. Right behind it was Declan's gray pickup. Getting out of her SUV, Aurora walked over to them.

Declan climbed out. "What are you doing? It's dangerous out here."

"I took care of that this afternoon. You don't have to worry anymore," Aurora assured him and walked around the car to Gardner.

Opening the door, she looked at her. She looked rough, her clothes rumples and her hair tangled. "Are you okay?"

When the girl didn't respond, Aurora did what she would do with

Win, she hugged her. Win needed to be hugged sometimes, though not so much now that she had Daniel.

"What do you think?" Declan asked as she hugged the girl tightly.

"To my place, for now. We can park her SUV in Win's spot. Let's leave your truck here. Let's go," Aurora said and went back to her SUV. "Rex, take Nick back to his vehicle. And I would keep me mouth shut if I were you."

Rex just gave her a dirty look as they walked away. She liked having dirt over people, and she didn't trust Rex all that much. Who was she kidding? She didn't trust many all that much.

With everyone safe, Aurora realized she suddenly had a little family, and they would need protection. No longer was it just Win or Win's little family. But she had two daughters, and she had to figure out what Declan meant to her. Was it enough to let him into her life? Would he want to be in her life after he found out about today? Not just about her mother but about Gardner.

CHAPTER
Thirty-One

AURORA CLIMBED into her SUV heading for home, with the man she loved following her with her adult daughter. This was going to be harder than anything she had done in years.

At her apartment, she waited as Declan parked Gardner's SUV. It wasn't a vehicle she had ever driven to the club, which was a good thing. It probably would have been stolen.

Gardner got out of the car, still looking like she was in shock, so Aurora took her hand and led her toward the building. Declan grabbed a box from the car and followed them to the elevators. On their floor, Aurora was suddenly lost. Now that they were here, she had no idea what to do with Gardner.

Where would she put her stuff? Her SUV was full of boxes, and they had to put them somewhere. Add to that, there was no bed for her. Millie was in the only other room. Would a woman raised like Gardner sleep on a couch?

"I'll order something for supper, for Win and Daniel also. Chinese?" she asked the room. Neither answered her, so she ordered it. If they were against it, they should have said so.

Once Daniel came home, Aurora was happy to see that Gardner

was playing with Millie, not eating the food that had arrived, but playing with her little sister, Aurora realized.

Taking another bite of rice, Aurora watched them. They looked nothing alike. Maybe they would have the same body type one day, but at this point, they both looked like their fathers and not much like her. As her mom, Aurora wished she had spent less time telling Gardner that she had little boobs and no butt. Mothers don't talk like that. Mothers tell their kids they are perfect.

The moment Win walked in the door, Aurora jumped to her feet and pushed Win back out the door across the hall and back into her apartment.

Win threw up her hands. "What? Can I eat?"

"Of course." Agreeing, Aurora went back to her place, grabbed some rice, chicken, and broccoli on a plate, then went back to Win's place. Not saying anything to those in the apartment as she did it.

"Here you are," Aurora stated, handing her the plate. Taking the plate, Win tried to sit at the table. "No, bathroom now."

"You're going to make me eat in a bathroom?" Win demanded but let herself be led there.

"Yes, now go." Aurora pushed her until they were in the master bathroom. Even with Daniel using the room, it was spotless. Winter was a perfectionist and liked to keep her spaces that way. The bathroom was cleaner than Aurora's entire apartment.

"I finally got the place clean after those girls," Win sat on the floor in her gray work skirt and jacket. The matching heels were missing. "What's up? We don't do bathroom chats much anymore. Are you knocked up again?"

"Fuck you, Winter."

"Fuck you, Aurora," Win said back, then took a bite of chicken.

"I figured out who Gardner's mother is today," Aurora admitted.

Win analyzed at a piece of broccoli on her fork. "Tiff?"

"I fucking wish." She added in a whisper, "Me."

Dropping her entire plate and fork, Win didn't even seem to notice when it hit the floor with a loud clatter. Rice, chicken, and broccoli went in every direction. "What did you just say?"

"You heard me." Aurora grabbed toilet paper to clean up the mess.

"How did you not know she was yours? That it was a possibility?" Win asked.

"Have you seen her, Winter? What about that says, my kid?" Aurora said

"How the fuck do you have a kid who is *twenty-three*?" Win asked because even if she knew her better than anyone else, they still didn't share everything.

"A fucking scheme of my grandma's. Selling a baby. I barely remembered it. I really blocked it out. She was born a few weeks before I got caught in the lab. Once I was in reform school, things changed for me. For the better." Aurora leaned her head back and closed her eyes.

Win sat down next to her and wrapped an arm around her. "You never said anything, even when you had Millie."

"Blocked it, Winter. I didn't even know if it was a boy or a girl. She was born at grandma's apartment. She gave me something, and I don't remember anything for days after. Nothing," Aurora admitted. She also hadn't pushed to try and remember. She'd never wanted to.

"So, you have a kid. What is she like?" Win was cleaning up the rice from the floor.

"She's Gardner, Winter. She's bubbly and excited about things. I think she's smart." Aurora shrugged.

"I like her. She didn't get her personality from you." Win smiled and reached for more toilet paper to clean more.

Aurora grinned. "Or her body type.".

"Or your tits," Win teased as she picked up a piece of broccoli and tossed it in the trash.

"Or my wit," Aurora surmised.

"But she landed herself a pretty good mom," Win said softly, no teasing this time.

"I have no idea what to do with her," Aurora admitted.

"Have you puked yet?"

"No."

"Which means you're doing better than last time," Win said with a laugh.

"Fuck you, Winter," Aurora said.

"I'm knocked up if that helps any. Our kids will be, what, twenty-four years apart in age." Win laughed because it was ridiculous.

"Of course, you tell me today."

"It's birth announcement day, Aurora," Win said. "Have you talked to her? Does she know you know?" Win asked.

"No, I have too. She's in shock. Her dad disowned her today."

"Bastard, but at least we don't have to share her for holidays."

"But she was raised as a fucking princess. How can I compete with that?"

"Don't disown her," Win suggested with a smile. "Treat her like Millie. Well, don't carry her around as much."

"Thanks for the advice," she said sarcastically.

"Just go talk to her. Send Declan to my place. You need to be alone." Win said, getting up. Her entire outfit had little grease stains from the rice falling on it, but the floor was actually clean. Anal Winter, at it again.

With a hug, Aurora left the bathroom and went to her apartment, where she promptly kicked everyone out, everyone she hadn't birthed, that is. Those she birthed didn't even seem to notice they had been singled out.

"Gardner?" Sitting down on the couch, Aurora smiled when she looked up from Millie's toys. She tapped the couch for her to sit next to her.

Reluctantly, the girl got up and sat on the other end of the couch from her. Her posture was stiff, and it only got worse when she noticed that they were alone. She was suddenly on edge.

"What happened today, Gardner?" In reality, she liked it on her better than the Gardi name. She seemed like a Gardner type person.

Gardner looked out the window at the city beyond. "My father decided I was not worth it anymore."

"He's a fucker. You know that, right? If he can't love you through thick and thin, he doesn't deserve you. Winter's dad did that when she was fifteen. He, too, is a fucker."

"He made me sign away any inheritance from him," Gardner admitted what Declan had told her.

"He left you destitute? You're a princess," she exclaimed in disbelief.

Her eyes came back to Aurora's. "I have money from my mom's family, Gardner money."

"Is that like play money, or was her name Gardner?"

"Her maiden name was Gardner. She died years ago. Her money has always been mine."

"So, you're okay for money?" Aurora asked again because she needed the confirmation.

"Yes. I'll find a place tomorrow. And I'll start looking for a job too," Gardner said,

"Up to you. Only you know how much money you have and how long you can live without a job. I'll always have something for you. If you need it." She said the last bit a little quieter. She had no idea what to do with her.

"Just not a stripper. Little tits." Gardner let out a little laugh at Aurora's words from months before.

"Gardner, if you want to strip, I won't stand in your way. I'm open-minded and flexible." Aurora lied but hoped she could change for this woman.

"Since when?" Gardner asked.

"Since I realized what a shitty person I have been to you since I met you. I don't want to be a shitty person to you." In some ways, she had treated her like her mom Debbie had treated her years before, stand-offish and far too critical.

"You have been okay. I'm not a stripper or a waitress." Gardner's voice cracked a little, but there were no tears in her eyes.

"You don't have to be a stripper or a waitress. There are other jobs. Better jobs, or different jobs anyway," Aurora tried.

"I don't need a job, Aurora. I think it would be better if I go to a hotel tonight." Gardner got up and picked up Millie and hugged her instead.

"Gardner, are you deaf?" Aurora watched her stop mid-hug with the baby and set her down.

Turning to her, Gardner answered, "Yes. It's inherited."

Aurora couldn't breathe, no blood tests were needed, and it didn't matter that the woman looked nothing like her. This was her daughter.

Another daughter she had given her mutant gene to. Another daughter whose life was awful because of her.

"Millie too. We had her tested last week. How did you know?"

"I just spent four years in college with a focus on deaf children. She doesn't mimic sounds, she doesn't track voices, she isn't talking yet, and since she only deals with adults, she should have picked up speech early." What she didn't say was that they had the same genes that could cause it, making Gardner more focused on it. She had been looking for it.

"How do you hear if you're deaf? You can hear, right?" Aurora asked because she didn't know. Maybe the woman was more gifted than Aurora had ever imagined.

With one hand, Gardner pulled back her thick brown hair to reveal hearing aids behind her ears. "I've had them since I was her age."

"How will I keep hearing aids in? She pulls on everything." Aurora said, looking at her handsy baby, even now pulling on Gardner's necklace.

"Mine are actually different than hearing aids. They are implanted into my head. They're what Millie will need. But they let you hear, she will hear," Gardner assured her, then kissed the baby's cheek.

"Thank you, Gardner. It would have gone under the radar for a long time if you hadn't pointed it out. I owe you." Aurora wanted to hug her but knew that they weren't there with their relationship. Might never be there.

"You don't owe me anything. I had fun working for you." Gardner put Millie on the ground. The little girl pouted a bit.

"You did not," Aurora said, watching her.

"Well, thank you again, and thank Declan for me. See you around." Picking up the one box Declan had carried into the apartment, she walked out.

Aurora stared at the door as it shut. She had just let her daughter walk away from her. It had been easy, too easy. But she let it happen because she didn't know how to be a mom. Looking at Millie on the floor, she realized she hadn't known how to be a mom to her in the beginning either, but now she was killing it. Except Millie wasn't a twenty-three-year-old princess who had nothing in common with her.

She had made it this far without her in her life; she wouldn't miss her in it now.

But now Aurora knew about her and was worried about her. What if she found some sleazy hotel and she was robbed? Her car was super expensive. Or if she was unable to find a place to live and had to live in her car? Where would she live if the car was stolen? There was nobody to catch her if she fell.

What the hell, she was falling *now*.

Bolting off the couch, she saw the hallway was empty. Pounding on Win's door, she yelled at them that she was leaving Millie alone. Running down the hallway, she waited for the elevator as Declan walked toward her as Win went to get the baby from Aurora's apartment. Declan was only halfway to her when the doors swooshed open, and Aurora jumped in and pushed the button for the garage and the door shut button.

Silently, she demanded that the elevator not stop on its way down. She needed to catch her kid. She was falling. Pacing back and forth in the tiny elevator, she pounced out of it when the door finally opened to the garage level. It was quiet. Running to the spot where Win's old brown Buick used to live, she saw Gardner loading her lone box back into her SUV.

"You can't go to a hotel. You'll stay here. Forever if you have to." She didn't even think; she just spoke. Her daughter needed a home, and damn it, she would give her one.

"No, I'm fine. You don't want me around." The girl had definitely gotten Aurora's stubborn streak, just like all her other bad genes.

"Fuck you, Gardner," Aurora said, maybe a little too harshly.

"What?" Her green eyes looked at Aurora in shock and pain.

"I said fuck you, Gardner, but I don't mean it," Aurora said in frustration.

"Okay." The kid bit her bottom lip as her shoulders slumped. Silently, she turned and opened the driver's door of her SUV.

"No, damn it. You can't leave. I have no fucking idea what to say to you." Aurora couldn't do this. She was messing up and had no way to get back on track.

"You don't have to say anything." She got into the driver's seat because, so far, Aurora hadn't said anything that made her want to stay.

Grabbing the door before it closed, she said the words she never thought she would have to say. Telling a story she had never wanted anyone to know, much less an innocent Gardner. "I was thirteen fucking years old, Gardner. I'd done things with men you still don't know about, all for money. I didn't want to, but to my grandma and my mom, it was easy money. So, when I got to reform school and away from them, I blocked it all out. I changed. Then I met Win, and together, we moved past who we were before we were arrested."

She took another breath, needing Gardner to hear it all. "Until I got pregnant with Millie, I never wanted kids. Hell, I never even thought about them. I know how to be a mom to a one-year-old, but you're not one anymore. I can't begin to imagine what you will want from me."

"I don't know what I want from you," Gardner said from inside the car, the door still open. It seemed they were both lost here.

Letting the door go, she watched Gardner let go of the handle. "Can we try and figure this out together? I know what it is like to be alone in the world. I don't want that for you. I want you to always have me."

"You don't have too, I'm fine."

"No, you're not. Me neither. I'm not good at this mom thing, with Millie I've gotten lucky. I don't see any examples of good parenting growing up. My mom was, well lets just say more interested in anything other than me.

"She didn't act like any grandmothers I've seen before." Gardner admitted.

Her words solidified Debbie's entire plot. She had never been interested in getting to know her granddaughter, her only goal was to use her anyway possible. Nobody deserved to be treated like that, much less someone like Gardner.

"You won't have to worry about her anymore after today. I shot her." She tried not to actually smile, because it still felt good. That look of surprise from the woman would live in her memory for a long time.

Gardner's green eyes widened in disbelief. "Dead?"

"I wish. Just in the shoulder, but they will arrest her and put her in jail for a long time. I'm glad you weren't too attached to her," Aurora said, leaning against her own car next to Gardner's open door.

"No, she was a bit… something."

"The eyes," Aurora said with a grunt.

Gardner nodded in agreement. "I haven't talked to her in over a month. She's called, but I haven't answered. I really didn't have anything to say to her and she just rambled about nothing."

"Good, she was blackmailing Paul King and me. The only thing she managed to do was drive King over the edge and piss me off. In the end, I won." Aurora said. "How did you find out who your father was?"

"Through a DNA testing site. That's how I met Debbie also, my grandmother. She told me I was yours," Gardner said.

With that, it all made sense. Because there was no way Debbie would have known who the father of Aurora's baby had been. The woman hadn't even known who Aurora's father was, and she had been there for that conception.

"A scam a minute with that one." Aurora chuckled, then asked, "Did she know who you were? I mean, that your parents are rich?"

Because if her mom had known Gardner had money, she would never have come after King or her. The Westmoreland's had more money than both combined five times over. So why the chump change instead of the big windfall?

"No, I didn't say much about me, and she didn't ask to many questions. She was more concerned about finding Paul King since she already knew where you were. Knew that you owned strip clubs. It was her idea for me to work for both of you before telling you who I was."

"That's Debbie for you. She tried to black mail two people with almost nothing and misses out on the fact that you come from millions.." Aurora smiled at her mom, who never changed. "What happens with you being disowned?"

"I really didn't belong there anyway. Dad has a second wife with new kids. He likes them better and always has. He never liked me; my mom did, but she died," Gardner said, a very condensed version of her story.

"Well, I like you, a little too bubbly, and you don't swear enough, but I can train you." Aurora smirked and held out her hand.

Aurora watched as Gardner looked at the offered hand. Was she ready to be caught yet? Could Aurora really be there for someone who wasn't Winter or Millie? She hoped she could be because her daughter needed her more than Winter did since Daniel showed up.

"What if you get tired of me? People do," Gardner asked tentatively, and Aurora wanted to beat every person Gardner had ever met and some she hadn't. Nobody picks on her babies!

"You get that from me, baby. People get tired of me all the time. But our family is different. With them, you can just tell them to fuck you. Because it means that I hate you right now, but I'll love you forever." Aurora wiggled her fingers at her, her hand still waiting for Gardner's.

"Always?" she asked, looking at the hand but not taking it.

"For people I know well. Mostly Winter and now Daniel, maybe Declan. You for sure." Aurora's arm was getting tired of waiting for her daughter, but she would wait for her.

Finally, Gardner took Aurora's and slid from her car. "Are you sure?"

"About eighty-five percent sure. The rest will come with time," Aurora said as she closed her daughter's car door and pulled her to the elevator.

"Are you dating Declan?" Gardner asked.

"Dating? Having hot sex? A little of both." Even Gardner could see Aurora was in too deep with this guy. That he was different than anyone else

"His company has been following me for months now," Gardner said innocently.

"You knew?" Aurora pushed the button to go up.

"Yes, they were always there. Always. Hot guys with guns are hard not to see." Gardner blushed at the admission.

"See, you are my kid." Aurora actually hugged her. Gardner hadn't gotten her body or her looks, but she had definitely gotten her brains. Possibly even more brains than Aurora had.

"So, are you two going to keep seeing each other now that he isn't being paid to guard me?"

"I think so. I haven't been able to shake him this week. But let's see how he reacts to the fact that I have a secret kid. Well, we both kind of have a secret kid."

He had Millie, after all.

"You mean Reese? I thought you already knew." Gardner just became second in command in the family.

Hugging her to her side, Aurora chuckled, "Your great grandma would have loved you, Gardner, fun name, observant, and fucking innocent as hell."

"What was mr Great-grandma's name?" Gardner asked. It seemed Debbie hadn't given her the entire family tree.

"Sylvia, and don't name your kids after her. She was a grizzly old bitch, used to throw knives at you if you walked in front of the TV," Aurora said as the elevator opened on the 25th floor.

Win was standing in the hallway, leaning against the wall, waiting. Nothing was said as Aurora and Gardner walked up to her. Stopping, Aurora introduced them, "Winter, my kid. Kid, Winter."

"No name, Aurora?" Win raised an eyebrow.

"Gardner, or are we changing it?" Aurora looked at her daughter, wondering what upbeat name she would choose that Aurora would hate instantly.

"Gardner. Gardner Ellsworth." She held out her hand as if they were actually meeting for the first time.

Win took the hand and leaned toward Gardner. She asked in a whisper, "What is your mom's real name?"

"Fuck you, Winter," Aurora stated.

"Fuck you, Aurora. I know everything about you. Why not this?" Win demanded.

"Don't ever tell, or you're out of the will," Aurora threatened Gardner as though Gardner didn't have way more money than Aurora did.

Win nodded at the door. "Declan's with Millie."

Everyone knew it was time to have that conversation. But Aurora had no idea where to start, when to start, or how to start. Just that by the end, Declan might be out of her life.

Thirty~Two

DECLAN CHECKED THE TIME. It had been forever since Aurora had left in the elevator. Win had demanded that he stay up here with the baby. He wasn't going to go against Win; she knew Aurora better than anyone else.

So here he was in her kitchen, cleaning up the Chinese food with one hand as he held his daughter in his other. Her little head was resting on his shoulder as she watched him work. Next week, they would find out what could be done to get her hearing fixed. Soon, he would have to tell Reese she had a sister, but first, he had to tell Millie's mom he was the dad. What an odd conversation that was going to be and she was no doubt going to be upset.

Once the kitchen was clean, he took the baby to look out the window at the city. If things went well with his conversation with Aurora, this could be his home. He knew Aurora wouldn't leave as long as Win was across the hallway. They were too close, which meant he would have to give up his house. Letting Reese live there alone was an easy decision as long as he moved in with Aurora and their daughter. It would take some getting used to the ease with which the neighbors came over and made themselves at home. But Aurora and Win had lived together for so long that the line of separation was still blurry. At least Daniel also felt that way.

It seemed odd that he was alone in her apartment. He had been alone here so little. But his call from Rex stating that Aurora had actually solved the case and had gotten the shooter arrested this afternoon had floored him. Also, the culprit was her own mother, whom she had shot. This woman was completely unpredictable.

But the lines still were not there for him. How she had connected the dots to her own mother was beyond him. Or had there been no dots at all, just his case, and she stumbled over her mom's plans? Maybe she was right, and he sucked at this job, though this case was the only one he had been so stupid at for years.

Aurora pushed through the door, and she had Gardner in tow. He was sure Gardner had left, that Aurora had probably kicked her out. She had admitted she hated having too many people in her apartment. But here she was, back again.

"Declan, you need to carry up that box again. We left it in her car," Aurora said as if they were in the middle of a conversation about it.

Aurora dismissed him and turned to Gardner. "Do you want to sleep on the couch, or I can get Xander's mattress for Millie's room? But you have to hurry. It's Friday."

"What are you talking about?" Declan was not going to let her take control this time. Now that the case was over, they had things that needed to be discussed.

"Sex night. Friday is Daniel and Win's sex night. Not that they don't have sex other times I'm sure, but Friday is special." Exasperated, Aurora explained, not answering the right question.

"Is Gardner staying?" he asked in confusion. Since the case was over, he could send her to his place, and she could stay with Reese. No need to have her in the next room.

Aurora pushed her toward the door. "Yes, Gardner, go get the mattress before they start."

"For how long?" Declan asked because she was, in fact, a grown woman.

"For as long as she wants to. I'm here when she falls, and she's falling," Aurora explained, but the answer made no sense to him.

"They had it waiting." Gardner dragged the air mattress into the apartment. She gave Aurora a weary look as if she didn't know if she wanted to be there.

"Winter, she's so on top of everything. Just bring it down to Millie's room," Aurora said and then grabbed her daughter from him, "Millie, you're having a sleepover. Your very first sleepover."

Gardner didn't say anything as she dragged the mattress to Millie's room and slammed the door. It seemed she needed space as much as Aurora did.

"Maybe we should talk about this." Declan tried to take control of the conversation. They needed to talk and not with Gardner in the apartment. He was sure there would be yelling. "I can call Reese to come and get her. They can go to my place until Gardner gets her feet under her."

Of course, he had brought the younger woman here, but he hadn't really wanted her to stay forever. Just until they knew she was safe. But now that she was, the apartment was too small for all these people, and his place was big and empty right now.

"No, she'll stay here," Aurora said, dismissing his plan completely. She was oddly happy about having her space invaded after a week of trying to get rid of every one of them all the time.

"Isn't it going to be a little cramped in here?" Declan hinted.

"I guess you could go; that would leave some room for the rest of us," Aurora pointed out.

"Are you kicking me out?" he asked because it sounded like she was trying to get rid of him and not the kid.

"Nope, but if you can't take me and mine, you can leave."

"You and yours? She isn't yours. You're not responsible for her. Not anymore," he stated the obvious.

"That's where you're wrong. I'm the mother she was looking for." She held Millie tight to her, too tight since the baby started to squirm.

"Bullshit." No fucking way was she the mother of a twenty-three-year-old! And even if she was, why hadn't she said earlier when they were trying to find the mother?

"Fuck you." She turned from him and walked toward Millie's room.

Doing some quick math in his head, he whispered to her, "Thirteen?"

Aurora stopped short. "So, what, Declan? Some of us didn't have the fun childhood that you had."

"Why didn't you tell me days ago?" he demanded. It would have made this case go a little smoother if she had just said something instead of hiding it from everyone.

"I didn't know then. I had forgotten, I was fucking thirteen." Her voice was low, so low he barely heard her. The anger of a moment ago was gone. The brash, cocky woman was gone. He saw the scared girl she once was in her words.

"You don't forget anything." He forced his words to be calm, to match her.

"I have spent a lifetime trying to forget the entire first decade and a half of my life." Aurora kissed Millie's head.

"Are you going to do blood tests?" He wanted to pull her into his arms and make it go away, but the reminder was in the bedroom behind him. All grown up and needing her, them.

"She already did, so I don't have to." She shrugged.

"She could be lying."

"Gardner cannot lie, you know that. And she carries the one gene that cannot lie." She finally set Millie on the floor. The baby went to the basket of toys in the corner like she always did.

"Green eyes?" It was all that they had in common.

Aurora rolled her own green eyes at him. "She's deaf. That comes from me."

"A. the tests are not back yet, and B. Gardner isn't deaf," Declan stated. The kid could hear as well as he could, probably better. He had spent enough time with her to know that.

"Is the test going to show you passed your genes onto her, Declan?" she asked, her brashness returning, then coyly added, "Or is it John?"

"How did you figure it out?" He was shocked. For weeks, she hadn't given one hint that she knew the baby was his. Not once.

"You can't run a con on me."

"When did you know?"

"When you sat across from me applying for a job. I look into those eyes every day, Declan. Why didn't you have the balls to tell me?" Aurora demanded, her own eyes constantly going to the baby in question like she expected him to pick her up. Like she was daring him to.

"I was waiting for you to be safe." Even to him, the excuse came out lamely. He knew he should have told her the moment he knew she existed.

"I'm always safe." Aurora held her arms out to her side as if to prove nothing could touch her.

"Because you shot your own mother." Declan watched her smile at his words, actually smile.

"It was the only way to stop her. She needed to be in prison long ago. I was doing society a favor. Everyone should be thanking me, throwing me a parade or something." The cockiness was back completely.

"Why was King trying to kill her?" If she knew all the answers, he would ask the questions.

"Because mommy dearest was blackmailing him. It drove him nuts. He was a pedophile. Remember, I was thirteen," she pointed out. He had forgotten that little detail. Or at least he had tried to forget that detail.

"Was she blackmailing you? Your mother?" he asked.

"Yes, but she was so bad at it I barely knew it was happening. She slashed the tires, classic Debbie. And I think she was the one behind us getting shot at. To try and scare me because I missed a money drop because she didn't mail it in time. Also, classic Debbie. My mom didn't get the master criminal gene." She shook her head in disbelief.

"Skipped her, went right to you," he pointed out.

"You got that right. Grandma was teaching me the business when I was in diapers."

"Pimping you out?"

"Fuck you. You're right. I don't remember the first time or which one of them thought of it first. But it was pretty old hat by thirteen. So, when you were in Little League, I was… Never mind, you know." She turned from him to look out at the city beyond the balcony that she had never been on.

"I get the picture." He did. He hated it. Hated that she had ever been so vulnerable that any of it had happened to her. He loved her as the brash ballbuster she was today.

"I also have stolen more cars in my time than you have ever even driven, and I was put in reform school at fourteen. I can hot-wire anything. Win's Buick hasn't had a key in eight years." She didn't look at him. She couldn't admit her crimes while facing him. It seemed some things she was too ashamed of.

"What put you there?" he asked, wondering if she had lied to him when she had told him before.

Aurora leaned back on the couch, "I told you, a Meth lab. It was Grandma's. I was just a dealer. But the lab got me sent away."

"You're a recovering drug addict also?" He needed all the information she would give because when she turned around, he knew it was over. She would be done talking.

"No, I never did them, alcohol a little, but not much. I don't do either because of Winter. She was a crackhead and drunk. She saved my life. I saved hers. Giving both up completely was the least I could do. Not to mention owning the club showed me the worst side of alcohol." Her words shocked him, not that he could see the woman across the hall as either of those things. That woman was as strong as this one, but their strength came from each other. Neither did it alone.

"And you sobered up before you were eighteen?"

"We've been sober since we were fifteen, thank you. So, cop, that is who is the mother of your child, well, the mother of one of them. She's possibly the mother of two of your children because your sperm fucking can't be contained. Do you spend all your days looking for children of yours because condoms don't work for you?"

She turned as she talked because he knew she wanted to see his face when she said the words. It was probably the deer-in-the-headlights look she expected based on her grin. But the tears were still there, making her cheeks shine, until she slyly wiped them with her sleeve.

"Two?" His mind was racing. It had only been two weeks. It was too early to know anything.

"I don't know if we should tell the baby that it was conceived in a parking lot at a strip club, but everyone has their stories, right? I mean, just because the last one was in a swanky hotel room means nothing. And this one might be deaf also. I mean, three for three, right?" She made her jokes, but the worry was in her eyes.

She was worried that he wouldn't want any of what she had to offer once he knew everything about her past.

"When were you going to tell me?" Racing to her, he grabbed her into his arms, showing her he was going nowhere, no matter what.

"Jeez, man, I haven't even told Winter, and she's way more important than you. And by the way, I tried to find you last time. Fake names are a turn-off." She let herself melt into him despite her words.

"No, they're not. Are you going to turn into a soccer mom?" he whispered into her neck, smelling her, loving her.

"Probably." She threw her head back in a laugh as if she just imagined it.

"Are you going to marry me?" Taking advantage of her neck being bare to him, he rained kisses on it.

"No, but I'll shack up with you. The kids need you. I mean, soon we will have four, and I really like to fuck you." She ran her fingers through his hair and pulled his head back so she could kiss his lips.

He hovered over them, not letting her kiss him. "Because you love me?"

"That's what makes it so good." She tried to pull him again.

"Can you say it?" He held fast, not letting her have what she wanted.

"Oh, Declan, I love you so much." She used her best southern accent. Which wasn't good at all, but she had said the words. One day, he knew she would be comfortable enough to say them in her actual voice. He would give her all the time in the world to become comfortable.

"I love you too, even if you're crazy." He let her kiss him finally, just once and quickly.

"I'm not crazy. I'm a business owner with skills." Her eyes were twinkling as she said it.

He didn't know how he was going to live with the craziness, but there was no way he wasn't going to. This was everything he had ever wanted and more. *Way more.*

Epilogue

WIN SMILED SO SWEETLY AS she looked at the new tiny baby in her arms. "The good news is we came up with a name for the baby while you were in labor, Rora. Thanks for taking so long. We needed all twenty-six hours to come up with something."

"We all can't have five-minute labors," Aurora grumbled at her best friend, who, not two weeks before, was the one in the hospital bed with the new baby. But she hadn't fought a war in it that lasted over a day. Aurora's new baby was sadly just as stubborn as all her kids were, just like their mom.

"Not my fault that I had a C-section." Win laid the baby on the bed and opened the blankets that were tightly wrapped around her.

Yup, another girl. Three for three, and within weeks, they would know if she was hearing impaired. This time, all they needed was a blood test to see if she had received the gene. Aurora was hopeful that this one would miss that gene. Because oddly, this baby had gotten a few more of them from her mom than her sisters.

Even now, at three hours old, her blonde hair was sticking straight up in the air, not the dark hair of Millie, even if it was the same style. Her eyes looked so much like Millie's already. Aurora knew they would be gray in a few months.

"You requested a C-section, and rich people get to do what they want," Aurora pointed out.

Though they didn't talk about money, they both knew that they were pretty even with income now that Declan had moved in. His business was better than Aurora had ever expected. What with how he fumbled Gardner's case, she thought he was just a bumbling detective. But he did okay and only every once in a while needed her help.

"The doctor requested it. Next time, you should go with him." It was the same fight they'd had since they first chose different doctors.

"No way am I going to a dude," Aurora stated her argument.

"I would rather have a dude than a lady sticking her fingers in certain places." Win wrapped the baby up again. An expert already with her two weeks of experience.

"I guess we can stop arguing it until next time." She took her baby back from Win, who had been hogging her own baby girl from her for weeks. So what if she could barely hold on to the little thing with her giant stomach?

Win wrinkled her nose. "There will be no next time. I'm done."

"Come on, you have to have two. Maybe another boy for Daniel."

"Nope, I'm too old for that," Win stated since they had both turned thirty-seven while pregnant.

"What's the real reason?"

"That." Win folded her arms. Since she was still on maternity leave, she was still in leggings and flannel shirts, forever the country girl.

"Liar." Aurora touched the blonde hair again, still not believing it.

"Sex, I haven't had sex in three and a half weeks. I'm not used to that long of a dry spell. Not again," Win admitted, as only Win would.

Aurora groaned. "That is a disappointing thought, not something I thought about with Millie. Thanks, now I'm depressed."

"What did you name her?" Win changed the subject.

"Aura." She grinned, loving it.

Declan had insisted the moment she was born. Until today, it was going to be Lauren Rose. For months, it had been. But today, he simply stated the baby was going to be named after her, and she had no say. Since she had named Millie, he got this one. Of course, she would have argued, except he'd named Aura after her because he said she looked just like her. She had added the Johanna since his pseudonym was John.

Win looked at the baby again, probably trying to see if the name matched. "Aura, cute."

"It is cute!" she hissed. "So, what amazing name did you come up with after two weeks?"

Win grinned. "Danielle."

"You didn't name your kid after your husband, did you? And that took two weeks?" Aurora demanded as if her baby wasn't named for her. Well, not directly, but it was the first name Declan knew her as.

"No, we named her the day she was born. We just didn't tell you until you named yours," Win admitted.

"You're a bitch."

"You don't even know her middle name yet."

"It's Aurora, isn't it?" she asked in disgust, but she had wanted them to name the baby after her since she had named Millie after Win.

Win smirked. "Nope."

"Hers is Rose, Aura Rose Chamberlin." She tipped the baby as if it would be written on her little tummy.

"Danielle Neveah McIntosh." Win grinned as if revealing a trick.

"Where did you come up with that one?" Aurora had never heard of it before. Maybe it was something from Daniel's family.

"Don't you know Aurora? Neveah is heaven spelled backward."

"Who told you?" she demanded and wished she hadn't just had a baby a few hours before and was still holding it.

"I have my ways of finding out things." Win took the baby from her again.

"I'll kill everyone who knows," Aurora hissed as Declan and Daniel came in the door, chatting about sports. Neither noticed the tension in the room.

"And I'll start with that one." She pointed at the man who had shared her bed and life for eight months. He knew too much and had to be silenced.

"What did I do?" Declan asked, all innocent.

"You told her. She was never to know, and you told her," Aurora insisted.

"I have no idea what I told her. But whatever it is, I'm sorry." Declan had started to just apologize when she was seven months pregnant. She might have turned bitchy in the end.

Win turned and handed him his daughter. "He didn't tell me."

"Get some paper. I'm writing Gardner out of the will. I told her from the beginning. Now, I'm not disowning her, just out of the will. She's still my daughter and will always be, but she needs to know there are consequences for spilling the beans." Aurora reached beside her but couldn't quite reach the pen.

"I don't think there's anything that you have that she cannot buy herself." Daniel handed her the pen from his pocket.

"I have stuff, Daniel. Really nice stuff. Stuff people want." Grabbing the pen, she tossed it onto the floor. She had nothing compared to Gardner, nothing.

"And she's a billionaire who has her own place." Declan cooed at his daughter.

It was true. Gardner was so loaded that she had bought Mrs. Grant's apartment for cash the day it went on the market. Apparently, the old woman had issues with the neighbors, but so far, Gardner hadn't complained about it. Maybe because she was able to take out her hearing aids at night.

"It wasn't Gardner," Win stated.

"Nobody else knows," Aurora argued.

Declan sat down on the bed and touched her cheek. "Knows what?"

"My name." She glared at him.

"Aurora, "no middle name," Carlyle," he said.

"My birth name," she hissed at him because he was acting stupid.

His eyes squinted at her. "I didn't know you had a birth name."

"Because you aren't good at your job."

"It's Heaven. I don't know if there was a middle name or not. I didn't hear it from either Declan or Gardner," Win said from across the room, no longer in the chair by the bed.

"Don't ever call me that. Ever," she hissed at her best friend.

"Settle down, Aurora. We will all agree to never call you that. Right?" he asked Daniel and Win.

"Sure," Daniel agreed.

"I'll sign no such agreement. She might need to be taken down a peg or two once in a while." Win crossed her arms, standing her ground.

"Winter!" Declan's voice was harsh and raspy.

"Fine, I won't call her that again," Win reluctantly agreed, glaring at Declan. It was the first time either man had gotten involved in the friendship. The two fought and made up so fast and so regularly that neither had bothered to try.

"Thank you," Declan said, his eyes on her.

Aurora held back tears because he understood how just the name could hurt her. And he wasn't going to let anything hurt her, not ever again. He would protect her, even when she didn't think she needed it.

"Love you," she whispered, not taking her eyes off him.

"Love you too, my Aurora."

"Okay, we are leaving," Daniel stated, but neither looked at him.

"Yes, we will. And I learned it from your mom. She doesn't like prison, and prison doesn't like her," Win told her as they walked out of the room.

The door softly clicked before Aurora stated, "I can take care of myself, especially with Win."

"I know. You're the strongest woman I know. But sometimes, I just want you to know that you don't have to be the strongest woman I know."

Staring at him, she tried to get him to turn away, to let her win the battle of wills. But he didn't, which made her love him a little more.

"You're beautiful, Aurora." He sounded choked up.

"I look like shit. I just spent a day battling your kid." She sat up and touched Aura again. Their baby—and they were together for it this time.

"You're both beautiful. And I love you both more than anything, and the three kids who are not here." He ran his fingers over her messy hair.

She looked into his grey eyes. "Do we really have four kids?"

"Yup, and in two apartments." Because when Gardner bought the place next door, she let Reese move in with her.

The house Declan had once owned had been sold, and the money had been put into college funds for the girls. Not for Gardner, who already had a degree, or Reese, whose college was being paid for by her new employer, her dad. But the two little ones that they were raising together. Which Aurora had to admit was easier than doing it on her own.

"My life is perfect." She sighed. Everyone she loved was in one place, just outside her door—or inside it.

"Our life is perfect, woman. Next time, I'm using my real name, so I don't miss so much time with you," he assured her.

"There will be no next time." She was never letting him go again. "You just have to make up that time with me now."

"I plan too. Every day," he promised.

They hadn't talked about marriage again, but they didn't need to. Life was perfect, just as it was. She was even looking at another club to buy. It was a small one, but she was ready to grow her empire again. With Declan by her side, she knew nothing could stop her.

Declan knew everything she had always kept to herself, and he had stayed. Not just stayed, but burrowed his way into her life. Exactly where she wanted him.

Bonus Epilogue

A YEAR AND A HALF LATER…

Aurora peeked outside the elevator and looked into the hallway. It was empty. Which was what she was looking for. She didn't need a lecture now, not from anyone. It was late, and she should have been home hours ago, but sometimes strippers needed a friend and not a strict boss. So she had gone out with them.

Declan had plans with Reese tonight, big plans, baseball plans. And the game had surely started already. Which meant she was in trouble. Or he would finally leave her, which she couldn't blame him for. She was hard to live with. Always had been.

She knew she could have had him drop their girls with Win and Daniel, but it was Friday, and they had plans. Gardner was watching Danielle for the night as usual. The kid couldn't say no to anyone, so Aurora tried not to ask.

Gardner had more Sylvia in her than Aurora would ever have thought because when she decided she wanted the apartment next door, she had gone over with a plate of cookies and had gotten them to sell her the apartment.

What the woman had said, Aurora would never know, but the couple had moved out within a week. Rumor had it they had moved to

Miami or Phoenix, someplace old people move, but Aurora had thought she saw them weeks later in the lobby of the building. But she hadn't managed to get their attention, and she had been yelling when she tried.

Reese had finally finished college. She had wanted to be a cop, and nothing was going to stop that. Well, only being the daughter of a PI had stopped that. She had been working for her dad ever since she got the job at the strip club. In the end she never even applied with the department, just started full-time with her dad.

That entire family was still on the top floor of Enderson, even if the two grown women were enjoying being single, and Aurora was the only one who had to listen to Declan complain about that. She preferred him ranting and raving about his daughters love life to her, and not to his daughter. But since they worked together, Reese probably heard it too.

Win poked her head out of Gardner's apartment. "Aurora, there you are. Where have you been?"

"What are you doing over there?" Ignoring the question, Aurora asked one of her own as if that would keep her out of trouble.

"Didn't you get the text?" Win came out and shut the door behind her.

"No," she hedged. She'd turned off her phone when she thought Declan would contact her about not showing up when she said she would.

"Reese and Nick are dating."

"Really?"

They had been spending a lot of work time together despite Aurora telling Declan to keep them apart.

"They didn't want to tell anyone because of Gardner." Win leaned against the wall. She liked to gossip about their family now that it was so big.

Nick had set his eyes on Gardner the day she became a member of the family. It didn't hurt that she was gorgeous and rich. Nick seemed like the type to appreciate money and looks.

After eighteen months, Gardner's 'father' hadn't come around, but she had gotten her finances straight and completely separated from the

Westmoreland's. She was now officially an Ellsworth. Though she would forever act and be a Westmoreland.

That was not strictly true; Gardner was the most down-to-earth person Aurora knew, and that was saying something. Aurora knew a lot of people. But that didn't mean the girl was anything like Aurora, which was for the best.

Even after all this time, Aurora still barely knew what to say to her and had yet to figure out how to mother her. She was, after all, an adult who had a head on her shoulders. Her life was more organized than Aurora's was.

Gardner bought her apartment and furnished it in three days. It had taken Aurora months to get everything she needed for her place. Gardner had matching dishes and special cups for tea. They even had saucers. Who had that?

Her daughter did.

She also had bath salts and paintings worth thousands, not to mention she was the first of the family to put up a Christmas tree, and it was real every year. No fake things for her. Decorated it like she was a professional.

All the while, she had been working at a local school as a teacher. Though she didn't have to work, she worked tirelessly for those kids. And, of course, she worked with the hearing impaired. It was her specialty. Her kid was a saint.

But Aurora wasn't; she had been out on the town with the girls and had left her husband behind. And her kids, not the one with her own apartment, but the other two. Yes, their dad was with them, but she was supposed to be home so he could have some father-daughter time with his other daughter.

"Is Declan in there?" she asked, forcing herself not to care that Nick had moved on from Gardner to Reese, and she didn't like it. But they were adults, and she had no say in their lives.

"He's with the girls. Daniel and Danielle. Everyone but you." Win folded her arms, then demanded, "Where have you been?"

She copied the stance. "Out, I don't have to explain myself to you."

"No, you don't. But Declan deserves a few words." Win shook her head and went back into the apartment.

Her disappointment made Aurora feel bad, not just a little, either. She hated to let Win down. Since marrying Daniel, she had raised up her opinion of everyone, including Aurora, and she missed the mark more often now.

Steeling herself for what was going to happen, she followed her friend into the apartment. Though Gardner was a billionaire, you couldn't tell by her home. It was homey and comfortable, even with the expensive paintings. It was like walking into a hug every time Aurora walked in.

"You came, Aurora. Do you want something to drink? I have snacks if you're hungry." Gardner rushed her, crowding in on her. She was like an over eager puppy.

"No, I'm good, thanks." Aurora warded her off, but the disappointment on her face was noticeable to everyone.

"Aurora, you missed the big announcement." With Aura in his arms, Declan handed her a bottle of water anyway, even if she didn't need it.

"Reese and Nick, I heard, congratulations." She lifted the bottle in the air as if in toast but knew she sounded anything but happy.

Looking over at Gardner, she wondered what she was feeling. The breakup had been a while back, but Nick dating her friend and roommate must have weighed on her since she hadn't dated anyone seriously since.

"Not that, about Gardner."

Declan wrapped his empty arm around Gardner and hugged her to him, even kissing the top of her head, which Aurora knew that Gardner loved a lot. She was an affectionate woman, something Aurora was not.

"What about Gardner?" she asked. Was she dating someone also? And when did you throw a party to announce that?

"I got a new job," Gardner said with the biggest smile on her face.

"You have a job." Aurora reminded her.

"This one is actually a paying job. Millie's school doesn't actually pay. I wanted a real job."

"Why? You don't need one," Aurora asked in confusion.

"I just want to be normal," Gardner argued, though her voice faltered.

"Princesses aren't normal."

Aurora instantly realized it was the wrong thing to say. Gardner's smile was gone.

"Don't call me that," she growled before spinning and running to her bedroom, slamming the door after her.

"Why do you always do that?" Win asked as everyone in the room stared at her.

"Do what?" She asked though she knew she had messed up.

"Treat her like she isn't your daughter," Win said low enough that Gardner couldn't hear her through the door.

"Just because I gave birth to her doesn't really make her my daughter," she hissed, tired of being the one who had to be the adult here. She hadn't asked for a full-grown kid to show up on her doorstep. She was doing just fine with her baby girl, now girls. They were easy.

"Why are you in such a bad mood tonight?" Declan asked as if he didn't know she was late getting home from work.

"Aren't you supposed to be at a ball game of some sort?"

"No, we decided to celebrate Gardner's new job instead. Because we are family." He pointed to the door she was now behind.

"Was that some sort of dig at me?" she demanded, needing a fight right now.

Win lifted an eyebrow. "Why don't you just go apologize?"

"Why do I need to apologize?"

Win gave her a little hug. "Because you're being a bitch, and this is a good day for your daughter. Congratulate her."

"Be human," Nick said from behind her.

Turning on him, she growled, "I don't need your help. In fact, the less I see of you, the better."

Sometimes, she couldn't control her emotions; after all, he had broken her daughter's heart. Even if he was now dating her stepdaughter, that didn't change anything. Gardner was simply too nice for her own good.

Knocking on the door, she opened it before there was a response. Gardner might not let her in if she waited for permission. Not that she had ever not let her in, but one day, it might happen, and today was a good day for it to start.

"Sorry, Gardner, I'm grumpy today," she admitted, though she stayed by the door. "Congratulations on the new job. Tell me about it."

Gardner looked up from the book she had been reading. She was leaning against the headboard with more than a dozen pillows behind her, protecting her delicate back from the hardwood of the headboard. As she spoke, she closed the book and set it on the nightstand.

The room was a mirror image of Aurora's, only in pastels and fluffy rugs.

"It's not far from Daniel's parents' house," Gardner said. "Special education."

Aurora couldn't understand why Gardner would want to move that far away. "What, that's like an hour's drive every day to get home."

Gardner shrugged. "Forty-five minutes if the traffic is good, but that won't be an issue."

"You're not taking the job?" Aurora was instantly relieved. She liked having her next door. It made being her mom easier when they saw each other all the time. Distance would make it all so much harder.

"I'm not driving every day. I'm renting an apartment not far from the school."

"No, you live here."

Gardner looked out the window for a moment before responding. "I need some space between me and Nick and Reese. Not saying I'm not happy for them, but I can't sit and watch it happen right in front of me. I'll come back on the weekends, but during the week, I'll stay there."

"Is this job more to do with Nick than with wanting to be paid?"

"It's both, Aurora."

"I don't like it." Aurora put her foot down. It was too soon for her to be leaving. There was supposed to be more time.

"It's not up to you to like or not. It's my life," Gardner told her and added, "We need some distance between us also. My living next door to you might have been a mistake. One that our relationship didn't need. Did we push too hard too soon for something that might not ever happen?"

Aurora shook her head. "No, because I already miss you not being here every day, and you aren't even gone yet."

Gardner didn't appear convinced. "You'll get used to it. I need to make my own way for a while. Teach kids who need me. The school I'll be working for hasn't had an ESL teacher in years, and there are students who need one. I'll be making a difference. It's what I want."

Aurora knew she was right and knew she needed to feel useful more than anything. "I support you, even if you don't need my support. And I'm always proud of you. I hope you know that."

"I do," Gardner said, and before she could say anything more, Aurora's phone went off with Declan's distinctive ring. "I think Declan needs to talk to you."

"Yeah, I might have blown him off to spend an evening with the girls."

"He understands. I know you don't think anyone does, but he does. He speaks fluent Aurora." Gardner got out of bed

"He speaks too much sometimes." She grinned at the thought that he actually knew her. "See you tomorrow, or are you already going to be gone?"

"I move next week. Found a great little place already."

"As usual. You're the planner."

"Someone has to. Now go home and eat some crow." Gardner pushed her toward the door.

Frowning, Aurora said, "That's a weird way to put it."

Gardner rolled her eyes. "I wasn't talking about sex."

"But you can, which you got from your mama!" Aurora grinned. She had worked hard to get Gardner out of her shell, even insisting on pole dance classes. And though Aurora didn't attend the actual class for long, she liked that Reese and Gardner did after they all ate fried food and talked at the club.

Gardner didn't answer as she pushed her out of the apartment. It was time to grovel. Which she knew she would have to do going into the night.

Even after all their time together, she was still testing him, seeing if this time he would give up on her and walk away. That she wasn't who or what he wanted anymore.

She just hoped he kept passing the test.

***

Declan laid little Aura in her crib and held his breath, hoping the move didn't wake her up. At six months old, anything could wake her unless you wanted her awake; then she was dead to the world.

Millie had gone down easy after a long day playing with Danielle. They had been so lucky that Daniel's mom had agreed to do daycare for Aura and Daniella at the same time. Everyone knew the woman was exhausted from her busy days, but the couples tried to limit her work week by only making her work a four-day week. That meant that someone in the two couples would take a day off each week, or Reese or Gardner in a pinch.

But sometimes she felt the domestic thing was too much for her. Like tonight when she hadn't answered his calls and had gone to a bar instead of coming home. He knew where she was the entire time because he tracked her phone. Something that would piss her off if she knew but gave him peace of mind. After all, her clubs weren't in the greatest neighborhoods.

These nights when she disappeared were happening less and less. He knew why she was doing it, even if he couldn't stop it. She needed to feel like she was in complete control of her life. That Declan and the girls didn't have a hold on her. It only lasted a few hours, but she rebelled in her own way.

The first time it had happened, he had panicked, sure that the relationship was over, that she was done with him. But she'd eventually come home and not said a thing about what had happened. She just went on like they had before. Now he could see when it was going to happen. This morning at breakfast, she had been combative and wouldn't commit to anything. Not even which club she was going to.

So he had canceled the ball game with Reese, which had turned out perfect because Gardner needed her family around for Reese's announcement. Her need for togetherness never ceased.

Declan knew Gardner far better than Aurora did. But then, Aurora was so worried about failing that she didn't put in enough effort. Every time Gardner needed approval and attention from her mom, Aurora failed, making Gardner feel rejected again.

Not that he was an expert on the woman, but he had raised a motherless girl and knew what to look for. Every time he had tried to give Aurora advice, she got mad and clammed up. So, he stopped even trying. Letting Win do what was needed because at least Aurora listened to her.

Slipping into bed, he left a low light for Aurora when she got home. She needed to talk to Gardner, and sometimes, those talks lasted a long time. Sometimes, they were over before they even started. Heart to hearts were not Aurora's strong suit.

Going over his latest case, he wondered why he had agreed to it. After the Westmoreland case, he started listening to his gut more and didn't take those he didn't trust. But this one was a cheating spouse, and he had proof. Sadly, he also had proof the man who had hired him was cheating. So, they were both in the wrong, and he was stuck in the middle.

"Are you still up?" Aurora had come into the apartment so quietly he hadn't even heard her. Which was what she did when she thought she was going to be in trouble. Something that she never was, but he knew there were things from her childhood that lingered.

"Yeah, wanted to see you before I went to bed."

"The girls are sleeping?" she asked.

"Yeah, went down easy."

"Are you mad at me?"

"No, I know you needed some Aurora time."

"What is Aurora time?"

"Whatever you do when you feel tied down. You spread your wings."

"You mad?"

"No."

"You missed the game," she said quietly.

"We had some family time instead, then Gardner had her little party."

"What did she make?"

"These things called cake pops. They are a cross between a cupcake and a sucker."

"Gross, glad I didn't notice."

"They were good. Cake on a stick is more like it. Then covered in frosting."

"Seems like a lot of work.

"Probably was. Gardner loves that, though."

Aurora sat down heavily on the bed. "She got some sucky job and is moving out."

"Because of Reese and Nick?"

"She said no, but probably. She fell hard for his savior persona."

"You don't think that's the real him?" he asked.

He had known Nick for years now, and he was a kind, considerate man. Someone he would want his daughter to date. Until his daughter started dating him.

Declan wasn't happy about tonight's news. He hadn't said anything, but Nick was far too old for his daughter. And after his and Gardner's breakup, Nick hadn't seemed overly concerned that he had broken the woman's heart.

"I saved her. He didn't do anything," Aurora stated angrily, which was true. Nick hadn't saved Gardner or Reese.

"You did. And are you still a tiny bit upset he dumped your baby girl?" he asked, knowing the truth.

"She dumped him, and yes. Gardner's perfect, and he threw that all away. No offense too Reese. She's perfect, too. He doesn't deserve her either."

"He doesn't."

"How did we end up with four perfect daughters? Us, who could have predicted that?"

He wrapped an arm around her. "Me, what else would we have? Imperfect? With you as their mom? Never."

Snuggling into him, she asked sadly, "How am I going to learn how to be her mom from across town?"

He pulled her closer. "You will just have to put more effort into it."

"That doesn't work, like practice, that never makes a person better.

It's natural talent or nothing," she complained, or argued, or whatever she did when things got hard and she didn't want to put in the work. Only this time, she had too. Gardner needed her too. Their family needed her to.

Instead of taking the bait, he told her, "Tell her you love her and that you aren't perfect. Maybe she will understand."

"But she already knows I'm perfect," Aurora grumbled.

"You keep believing that." He grinned at her frown. "Now, if I were you, I would help her move, get her a housewarming present, and most importantly, don't tell her she's making a mistake taking the job. She's very excited about it."

"I'm not saying you're right. I'm just saying I'll take your advice under consideration." She snuggled tightly into him. "Do you happen to remember when my daughter was in a serious relationship, and you kept telling me about how she was having a lot of sex just across the wall from here?"

It had been fun to see how annoyed Aurora would get. "Yeah."

"Turn around's going to be a bitch, isn't it?"

"I don't want to think about it."

He didn't like to think about his daughter being an adult.

"I bet they are doing it right now, just down the hall. And by it, I mean sex." Aurora giggled at her prediction.

Getting up, he lifted her into his arms and said, "The only sex I'm thinking about right now is sex with you."

"The best kind of sex there is." She willingly let him carry her to their bedroom. A room that hadn't changed since he moved in, except his clothes were in their shared closet.

She leaned her head against his shoulder. "Why aren't you mad at me?"

It had taken a long time for her to let her guard down completely with him. Time to let herself be content with the fact that she'd let him take care of her. He'd let her take all the time she needed because, in the end, he loved it when she did. Loved it because it showed him every time it happened that she loved him enough to trust him. And in the end, winning her love had been a lot easier than winning her trust.

He kissed her forehead. "Because you'll always come back, Aurora. This is where your home is now. With us."

The End

Thank you so much for reading more about Aurora and Declan. Did you love it? It would be greatly appreciated if you could drop a review so others can find and enjoy it.

About the Author

I love to read and prefer a little spice in those books. I'm lucky enough to live on a small hobby farm in northern Minnesota with my husband and two half grown kids. I enjoy spending time in the pasture with my two mini horses and one fainting goat (who doesn't actually faint). When I'm not writing, I'm busy trying to do all the things I didn't get to while writing. Or maybe I wouldn't have gotten to them anyway, because its laundry, dishes and fun things like that.

What to know more about me and my writing? You can sign up for my newsletter to get the scoop at my web site WWW.ALIEGARNETT.COM